I0566655

Philip K. Dick

In the Parallel Universe - 4 SF Tales in One Edition

OK Publishing 2021

Philip K. Dick
In the Parallel Universe - 4 SF Tales in One Edition

Adjustment Team, The Defenders, The Unreconstructed M & Breakfast at Twilight

Published by

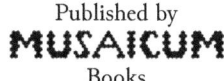

Books

- Advanced Digital Solutions & High-Quality book Formatting -

musaicumbooks@okpublishing.info

2021 OK Publishing

ISBN 978-80-272-7798-8

Contents

Adjustment Team

SOMETHING WENT WRONG…AND ED FLETCHER GOT MIXED UP IN THE BIGGEST THING IN HIS LIFE.

It was bright morning. The sun shone down on the damp lawns and sidewalks, reflecting off the sparkling parked cars. The Clerk came walking hurriedly, leafing through his instructions, flipping pages and frowning. He stopped in front of the small green stucco house for a moment, and then turned up the walk, entering the back yard.

The dog was asleep inside his shed, his back turned to the world. Only his thick tail showed.

"For Heaven's sake," the Clerk exclaimed, hands on his hips. He tapped his mechanical pencil noisily against his clipboard. "Wake up, you in there."

The dog stirred. He came slowly out of his shed, head first, blinking and yawning in the morning sunlight. "Oh, it's you. Already?" He yawned again.

"Big doings." The Clerk ran his expert finger down the traffic-control sheet. "They're adjusting Sector T137 this morning. Starting at exactly nine o'clock." He glanced at his pocket watch. "Three hour alteration. Will finish by noon."

"T137? That's not far from here."

The Clerk's lips twisted in contempt. "Indeed. You're showing astonishing perspicacity, my black-haired friend. Maybe you can divine why I'm here."

"We overlap with T137."

"Exactly. Elements from this sector are involved. We must make sure they're properly placed when adjustment begins." The Clerk glanced toward the small green stucco house. "Your particular task concerns the man in there. He is employed by a business establishment lying within Sector T137. It's essential he be there before nine o'clock.

The dog studied the house. The shades had been let up. The kitchen light was on. Beyond the lace curtains dim shapes could be seen, stirring around the table. A man and woman. They were drinking coffee.

"There they are," the dog murmured. "The man, you say? He's not going to be harmed, is he?"

"Of course not. But he must be at his office early. Usually he doesn't leave until after nine. Today he must leave at eight-thirty. He must be within Sector T137 before the process begins, or he won't be altered to coincide with the new adjustment."

The dog sighed. "That means I have to summon."

"Correct." The Clerk checked his instruction sheet. "You're to summon at precisely eight-fifteen. You've got that? Eight-fifteen. No later."

"What will an eight-fifteen summons bring?"

The Clerk flipped open his instruction book, examining the code columns. "It will bring A Friend with a Car. To drive him to work early." He closed the book and folded his arms, preparing to wait. "That way he'll get to his office almost an hour ahead of time. Which is vital."

"Vital," the dog murmured. He lay down, half inside his shed. His eyes closed. "Vital."

"Wake up! This must be done exactly on time. If you summon too soon or too late —"

The dog nodded sleepily. "I know. I'll do it right. I *always* do it right."

Ed Fletcher poured more cream in his coffee. He sighed, leaning back in his chair. Behind him the oven hissed softly, filling the kitchen with warm fumes. The yellow overhead light beamed down.

"Another roll?" Ruth asked.

"I'm full." Ed sipped his coffee. "You can have it."

"Have to go." Ruth got to her feet, unfastening her robe. "Time to go to work."

"Already?"

"Sure. You lucky bum! Wish I could sit around." Ruth moved toward the bathroom, running her fingers through her long black hair. "When you work for the Government you start early."

"But you get off early," Ed pointed out. He unfolded the *Chronicle*, examining the sporting green. "Well, have a good time today. Don't type any wrong words, any double-entendres."

The bathroom door closed, as Ruth shed her robe and began dressing.

Ed yawned and glanced up at the clock over the sink. Plenty of time. Not even eight. He sipped more coffee and then rubbed his stubbled chin. He would have to shave. He shrugged lazily. Ten minutes, maybe.

Ruth came bustling out in her nylon slip, hurrying into the bedroom. "I'm late." She rushed rapidly around, getting into her blouse and skirt, her stockings, her little white shoes. Finally she bent over and kissed him. "Goodbye, honey. I'll do the shopping tonight."

"Goodbye." Ed lowered his newspaper and put his arm around his wife's trim waist, hugging her affectionately. "You smell nice. Don't flirt with the boss."

Ruth ran out the front door, clattering down the steps. He heard the click of her heels diminish down the sidewalk.

She was gone. The house was silent. He was alone.

Ed got to his feet, pushing his chair back. He wandered lazily into the bathroom and got his razor down. Eight-ten. He washed his face, rubbing it down with shaving cream, and began to shave. He shaved leisurely. He had plenty of time.

The Clerk bent over his round pocket watch, licking his lips nervously. Sweat stood out on his forehead. The second hand ticked on. Eight-fourteen. Almost time.

"Get ready!" the Clerk snapped. He tensed, his small body rigid. "Ten seconds to go!"

"Time!" the Clerk cried.

Nothing happened.

The Clerk turned, eyes wide with horror. From the little shed a thick black tail showed. The dog had gone back to sleep.

"TIME!" the Clerk shrieked. He kicked wildly at the furry rump. "In the name of God —"

The dog stirred. He thumped around hastily, backing out of the shed. "My goodness." Embarrassed, he made his way quickly to the fence. Standing up on his hind paws, he opened his mouth wide. "Woof!" he summoned. He glanced apologetically at the Clerk. "I beg your pardon. I can't understand how —"

The Clerk gazed fixedly down at his watch. Cold terror knotted his stomach. The hands showed eight-sixteen. "You failed," he grated. "You failed! You miserable flea-bitten rag-bag of a wornout old mutt! You failed!"

The dog dropped and came anxiously back. "I failed, you say? You mean the summons time was —?"

"You summoned too late." The Clerk put his watch away slowly, a glazed expression on his face. "You summoned too late. We won't get A Friend with a Car. There's no telling what will come instead. I'm afraid to see what eight-sixteen brings."

"I hope he'll be in Sector T137 in time."

"He won't," the Clerk wailed. "He won't be there. We've made a mistake. We've made things go wrong!"

Ed was rinsing the shaving cream from his face when the muffled sound of the dog's bark echoed through the silent house.

"Damn," Ed muttered. "Wake up the whole block." He dried his face, listening. Was somebody coming?

A vibration. Then —

The doorbell rang.

Ed came out of the bathroom. Who could it be? Had Ruth forgotten something? He tossed on a white shirt and opened the front door.

A bright young man, face bland and eager, beamed happily at him. "Good morning, sir." He tipped his hat. "I'm sorry to bother you so early —"

"What do you want?"

"I'm from the Federal Life Insurance Company. I'm here to see you about —"

Ed pushed the door closed. "Don't want any. I'm in a rush. Have to get to work."

"Your wife said this was the only time I could catch you." The young man picked up his briefcase, easing the door open again. "She especially asked me to come this early. We don't usually begin our work at this time, but since she asked me, I made a special note about it"

"Okay." Sighing wearily, Ed admitted the young man. "You can explain your policy while I get dressed."

The young man opened his briefcase on the couch, laying out heaps of pamphlets and illustrated folders. "I'd like to show you some of these figures, if I may. It's of great importance to you and your family to —"

Ed found himself sitting down, going over the pamphlets. He purchased a ten-thousand-dollar policy on his own life and then eased the young man out. He looked at the clock. Practically nine-thirty!

"Damn." He'd be late to work. He finished fastening his tie, grabbed his coat, turned off the oven and the lights, dumped the dishes in the sink, and ran out on the porch.

As he hurried toward the bus stop he was cursing inwardly. Life insurance salesmen. Why did the jerk have to come just as he was getting ready to leave?

Ed groaned. No telling what the consequences would be, getting to the office late. He wouldn't get there until almost ten. He set himself in anticipation. A sixth sense told him he was in for it. Something bad. It was the wrong day to be late.

If only the salesman hadn't come.

Ed hopped off the bus a block from his office. He began walking rapidly. The huge clock in front of Stein's Jewelry Store told him it was almost ten.

His heart sank. Old Douglas would give him hell for sure. He could see it now. Douglas puffing and blowing, red-faced, waving his thick finger at him; Miss Evans, smiling behind her typewriter; Jackie, the office boy, grinning and snickering; Earl Hendricks; Joe and Tom; Mary, dark-eyed, full bosom and long lashes. All of them, kidding him the whole rest of the day.

He came to the corner and stopped for the light. On the other side of the street rose the big white concrete building, the towering column of steel and cement, girders and glass windows-the office building. Ed flinched. Maybe he could say the elevator got stuck. Somewhere between the second and third floor.

The street light changed. Nobody else was crossing. Ed crossed alone. He hopped up on the curb on the far side —

And stopped, rigid.

The sun had winked off. One moment it was beaming down. Then it was gone. Ed looked sharply up. Gray clouds swirled above him. Huge, formless clouds. Nothing more. An ominous, thick haze that made everything waver and dim. Uneasy chills plucked at him. *What was it?*

He advanced cautiously, feeling his way through the mist. Everything was silent. No sounds-not even the traffic sounds. Ed peered frantically around, trying to see through the rolling haze. No people. No cars. No sun. Nothing.

The office building loomed up ahead, ghostly. It was an indistinct gray. He put out his hand uncertainly —

A section of the building fell away. It rained down, a torrent of particles. Like sand. Ed gaped foolishly. A cascade of gray debris, spilling around his feet. And where he had touched the building, a jagged cavity yawned-an ugly pit marring the concrete.

Dazed, he made his way to the front steps. He mounted them. The steps gave way underfoot. His feet sank down. He was wading through shifting sand, weak, rotted stuff that broke under his weight.

He got into the lobby. The lobby was dim and obscure. The overhead lights flickered feebly in the gloom. An unearthly pall hung over everything.

He spied the cigar stand. The seller leaned silently, resting on the counter, toothpick between his teeth, his face vacant. *And gray.* He was gray all over.

"Hey," Ed croaked. "What's going on?"

The seller did not answer. Ed reached out toward him. His hand touched the seller's gray arm-and passed right through.

"Good God," Ed said.

The seller's arm came loose. It fell to the lobby floor, disintegrating into fragments. Bits of gray fiber. Like dust. Ed's senses reeled.

"Help!" he shouted, finding his voice.

No answer. He peered around. A few shapes stood here and there: a man reading a newspaper, two women waiting at the elevator.

Ed made his way over to the man. He reached out and touched him.

The man slowly collapsed. He settled into a heap, a loose pile of gray ash. Dust. Particles. The two women dissolved when he touched them. Silently. They made no sound as they broke apart.

Ed found the stairs. He grabbed hold of the bannister and climbed. The stairs collapsed under him. He hurried faster. Behind him lay a broken path-his footprints clearly visible in the concrete. Clouds of ash blew around him as he reached the second floor.

He gazed down the silent corridor. He saw more clouds of ash. He heard no sound. There was just darkness-rolling darkness.

He climbed unsteadily to the third floor. Once, his shoe broke completely through the stair. For a sickening second he hung, poised over a yawning hole that looked down into a bottomless nothing.

Then he climbed on, and emerged in front of his own office: DOUGLAS AND BLAKE, REAL ESTATE.

The hall was dim, gloomy with clouds of ash. The overhead lights flickered fitfully. He reached for the door handle. The handle came off in his hand. He dropped it and dug his fingernails into the door. The plate glass crashed past him, breaking into bits. He tore the door open and stepped over it, into the office.

Miss Evans sat at her typewriter, fingers resting quietly on the keys. She did not move. She was gray, her hair, her skin, her clothing. She was without color. Ed touched her. His fingers went through her shoulder, into dry flakiness.

He drew back, sickened. Miss Evans did not stir.

He moved on. He pushed against a desk. The desk collapsed into rotting dust. Earl Hendricks stood by the water cooler, a cup in his hand. He was a gray statue, unmoving. Nothing stirred. No sound. No life. The whole office was gray dust-without life or motion.

Ed found himself out in the corridor again. He shook his head, dazed. What did it mean? Was he going out of his mind? Was he —?

A sound.

Ed turned, peering into the gray mist. A creature was coming, hurrying rapidly. A man —a man in a white robe. Behind him others came. Men in white, with equipment. They were lugging complex machinery.

"Hey —" Ed gasped weakly.

The men stopped. Their mouths opened. Their eyes popped.

"Look!"

"Something's gone wrong!"

"One still charged."

"Get the de-energizer."

"We can't proceed until —"

The men came toward Ed, moving around him. One lugged a long hose with some sort of nozzle. A portable cart came wheeling up. Instructions were rapidly shouted.

Ed broke out of his paralysis. Fear swept over him. Panic. Something hideous was happening. He had to get out. Warn people. Get away.

He turned and ran, back down the stairs. The stairs collapsed under him. He fell half a flight, rolling in heaps of dry ash. He got to his feet and hurried on, down to the ground floor.

The lobby was lost in the clouds of gray ash. He pushed blindly through, toward the door. Behind him, the white-clad men were coming, dragging their equipment and shouting to each other, hurrying quickly after him.

He reached the sidewalk. Behind him the office building wavered and sagged, sinking to one side, torrents of ash raining down in heaps. He raced toward the corner, the men just behind him. Gray clouds swirled around him. He groped his way across the street, hands outstretched. He gained the opposite curb —

The sun winked on. Warm yellow sunlight streamed down on him. Cars honked. Traffic lights changed. On all sides men and women in bright spring clothes hurried and pushed: shoppers, a blue-clad cop, salesmen with briefcases. Stores, windows, signs ... noisy cars moving up and down the street...

And overhead was the bright sun and familiar blue sky.

Ed halted, gasping for breath. He turned and looked back the way he had come. Across the street was the office building-as it had always been. Firm and distinct. Concrete and glass and steel.

He stepped back a pace and collided with a hurrying citizen. "Hey," the man grunted. "Watch it."

"Sorry." Ed shook his head, trying to clear it. From where he stood, the office building looked like always, big and solemn and substantial, rising up imposingly on the other side of the street.

But a minute ago —

Maybe he was out of his mind. He had seen the building crumbling into dust. Building-and people. They had fallen into gray clouds of dust. And the men in white-they had chased him. Men in white robes, shouting orders, wheeling complex equipment.

He was out of his mind. There was no other explanation. Weakly, Ed turned and stumbled along the sidewalk, his mind reeling. He moved blindly, without purpose, lost in a haze of confusion and terror.

The Clerk was brought into the top-level Administrative chambers and told to wait.

He paced back and forth nervously, clasping and wringing his hands in an agony of apprehension. He took off his glasses and wiped them shakily.

Lord. All the trouble and grief. And it wasn't his fault. But he would have to take the rap. It was his responsibility to get the Summoners routed out and their instructions followed. The miserable flea-infested Summoner had gone back to sleep-and *he* would have to answer for it.

The doors opened. "All right," a voice murmured, preoccupied. It was a tired, care-worn voice. The Clerk trembled and entered slowly, sweat dripping down his neck into his celluloid collar.

The Old Man glanced up, laying aside his book. He studied the Clerk calmly, his faded blue eyes mild —a deep, ancient mildness that made the Clerk tremble even more. He took out his handkerchief and mopped his brow.

"I understand there was a mistake," the Old Man murmured. "In connection with Sector T137. Something to do with an element from an adjoining area."

"That's right." The Clerk's voice was faint and husky. "Very unfortunate."

"What exactly occurred?"

"I started out this morning with my instruction sheets. The material relating to T137 had top priority, of course. I served notice on the Summoner in my area that an eight-fifteen summons was required."

"Did the Summoner understand the urgency?"

"Yes, sir." The Clerk hesitated. "But —"

"But what?"

The Clerk twisted miserably. "While my back was turned the Summoner crawled back in his shed and went to sleep. I was occupied, checking the exact time with my watch. I called the moment-but there was no response."

"You called at eight-fifteen exactly?"

"Yes, sir! Exactly eight-fifteen. But the Summoner was asleep. By the time I managed to arouse him it was eight-*sixteen*. He summoned, but instead of A Friend with a Car we got a —A Life Insurance Salesman." The Clerk's face screwed up with disgust. "The Salesman kept the element there until almost nine-thirty. Therefore he was late to work instead of early."

For a moment the Old Man was silent. "Then the element was not within T137 when the adjustment began."

"No. He arrived about ten o'clock."

"During the middle of the adjustment." The Old Man got to his feet and paced slowly back and forth, face grim, hands behind his back. His long robe flowed out behind him. "A serious matter. During a Sector Adjustment all related elements from other Sectors must be included. Otherwise, their orientations remain out of phase. When this element entered T137 the adjustment had been in progress fifty minutes. The element encountered the Sector at its most de-energized stage. He wandered about until one of the adjustment teams met him."

"Did they catch him?"

"Unfortunately no. He fled, out of the Sector. Into a nearby fully energized area."

"What-what then?"

The Old Man stopped pacing, his lined face grim. He ran a heavy hand through his long white hair. "We do not know. We lost contact with him. We will reestablish contact soon, of course. But for the moment he is out of control."

"What are you going to do?"

"He must be contacted and contained. He must be brought up here. There's no other so-lution."

"Up *here!*"

"It is too late to de-energize him. By the time he is regained he will have told others. To wipe his mind clean would only complicate matters. Usual methods will not suffice. I must deal with this problem myself."

"I hope he's located quickly," the Clerk said.

"He will be. Every Watcher is alerted. Every Watcher and every Summoner." The Old Man's eyes twinkled. "Even the Clerks, although we hesitate to count on them."

The Clerk flushed. "I'll be glad when this thing is over," he muttered.

Ruth came tripping down the stairs and out of the building, into the hot noonday sun. She lit a cigarette and hurried along the walk, her small bosom rising and falling as she breathed in the spring air.

"Ruth." Ed stepped up behind her.

"Ed!" She spun, gasping in astonishment. "What are you doing away from —?"

"Come on." Ed grabbed her arm, pulling her along. "Let's keep moving."

"But what —?"

"I'll tell you later." Ed's face was pale and grim. "Let's go where we can talk. In private."

"I was going down to have lunch at Louie's. We can talk there." Ruth hurried along breath-lessly. "What is it? What's happened? You look so strange. And why aren't you at work? Did you-did you get fired?"

They crossed the street and entered a small restaurant. Men and women milled around, getting their lunch. Ed found a table in the back, secluded in a corner. "Here." He sat down abruptly. "This will do." She slid into the other chair.

Ed ordered a cup of coffee. Ruth had salad and creamed tuna on toast, coffee and peach pie. Silently, Ed watched her as she ate, his face dark and moody.

"Please tell me," Ruth begged.

"You really want to know?"

"Of course I want to know!" Ruth put her small hand anxiously on his. "I'm your wife."

"Something happened today. This morning. I was late to work. A damn insurance man came by and held me up. I was half an hour late."

Ruth caught her breath. "Douglas fired you."

"No." Ed ripped a paper napkin slowly into bits. He stuffed the bits in the half-empty water glass. "I was worried as hell. I got off the bus and hurried down the street. I noticed it when I stepped up on the curb in front of the office."

"Noticed what?"

Ed told her. The whole works. Everything.

When he had finished, Ruth sat back, her face white, hands trembling. "I see," she murmured. "No wonder you're upset." She drank a little cold coffee, the cup rattling against the saucer. "What a terrible thing."

Ed leaned intently toward his wife. "Ruth. Do you think I'm going crazy?"

Ruth's red lips twisted. "I don't know what to say. It's so strange..."

"Yeah. Strange is hardly the word for it. I poked my hands right through them. Like they were clay. Old dry clay. Dust. Dust figures." Ed lit a cigarette from Ruth's pack. "When I got out I looked back and there it was. The office building. Like always."

"You were afraid Mr. Douglas would bawl you out, weren't you?"

"Sure. I was afraid-and guilty." Ed's eyes flickered. "I know what you're thinking. I was late and I couldn't face him. So I had some sort of protective psychotic fit. Retreat from reality." He stubbed the cigarette out savagely. "Ruth, I've been wandering around town since. Two and a half hours. Sure, I'm afraid. I'm afraid like hell to go back."

"Of Douglas?"

"No! The men in white." Ed shuddered. "God. Chasing me. With their damn hoses and-and equipment."

Ruth was silent. Finally she looked up at her husband, her dark eyes bright. "You have to go back, Ed."

"Back? Why?"

"To prove something."

"Prove what?"

"Prove it's all right." Ruth's hand pressed against his. "You have to, Ed. You have to go back and face it. To show yourself there's nothing to be afraid of."

"The hell with it! After what I saw? Listen, Ruth. I saw the fabric of reality split open. I saw —*behind*. Underneath. I saw what was really there. And I don't want to go back. I don't want to see dust people again. Ever."

Ruth's eyes were fixed intently on him. "I'll go back with you," she said.

"For God's sake."

"For *your* sake. For your sanity. So you'll know." Ruth got abruptly to her feet, pulling her coat around her. "Come on, Ed. I'll go with you. We'll go up there together. To the office of Douglas and Blake, Real Estate. I'll even go in with you to see Mr. Douglas."

Ed got up slowly, staring hard at his wife. "You think I blacked out. Cold feet. Couldn't face the boss." His voice was low and strained. "Don't you?"

Ruth was already threading her way toward the cashier. "Come on. You'll see. It'll all be there. Just like it always was."

"Okay," Ed said. He followed her slowly. "We'll go back there-and see which of us is right."

They crossed the street together, Ruth holding on tight to Ed's arm. Ahead of them was the building, the towering structure of concrete and metal and glass.

"There it is," Ruth said. "See?"

There it was, all right. The big building rose up, firm and solid, glittering in the early afternoon sun, its windows sparkling brightly.

Ed and Ruth stepped up onto the curb. Ed tensed himself, his body rigid. He winced as his foot touched the pavement —

But nothing happened: the street noises continued; cars, people hurrying past; a kid selling papers. There were sounds, smells, the noises of the city in the middle of the day. And overhead was the sun and the bright blue sky.

"See?" Ruth said. "I was right."

They walked up the front steps, into the lobby. Behind the cigar stand the seller stood, arms folded, listening to the ball game. "Hi, Mr. Fletcher," he called to Ed. His face lit up good-naturedly. "Who's the dame? Your wife know about this?"

Ed laughed unsteadily. They passed on toward the elevator. Four or five businessmen stood waiting. They were middle-aged men, well dressed, waiting impatiently in a bunch. "Hey, Fletcher," one said. "Where you been all day? Douglas is yelling his head off."

"Hello, Earl," Ed muttered. He gripped Ruth's arm. "Been a little sick."

The elevator came. They got in. The elevator rose. "Hi, Ed," the elevator operator said. "Who's the good-looking gal? Why don't you introduce her around?"

Ed grinned mechanically. "My wife."

The elevator let them off at the third floor. Ed and Ruth got out, heading toward the glass door of Douglas and Blake, Real Estate.

Ed halted, breathing shallowly. "Wait." He licked his lips. "I —"

Ruth waited calmly as Ed wiped his forehead and neck with his handkerchief. "All right now?"

"Yeah." Ed moved forward. He pulled open the glass door.

Miss Evans glanced up, ceasing her typing. "Ed Fletcher! Where on earth have you been?"

"I've been sick. Hello, Tom."

Tom glanced up from his work. "Hi, Ed. Say, Douglas is yelling for your scalp. Where have you been?"

"I know." Ed turned wearily to Ruth. "I guess I better go in and face the music."

Ruth squeezed his arm. "You'll be all right. I know." She smiled, a relieved flash of white teeth and red lips. "Okay? Call me if you need me."

"Sure." Ed kissed her briefly on the mouth. "Thanks, honey. Thanks a lot. I don't know what the hell went wrong with me. I guess it's over."

"Forget it. So long." Ruth skipped back out of the office, the door closing after her. Ed listened to her race down the hall to the elevator.

"Nice little gal," Jackie said appreciatively.

"Yeah." Ed nodded, straightening his necktie. He moved unhappily toward the inner office, steeling himself. Well, he had to face it. Ruth was right. But he was going to have a hell of a time explaining it to the boss. He could see Douglas now, thick red wattles, big bull roar, face distorted with rage —

Ed stopped abruptly at the entrance to the inner office. He froze rigid. The inner office-it was *changed*.

The hackles of his neck rose. Cold fear gripped him, clutching at his windpipe. The inner office was different. He turned his head slowly, taking in the sight: the desks, chairs, fixtures, file cabinets, pictures.

Changes. Little changes. Subtle. Ed closed his eyes and opened them slowly. He was alert, breathing rapidly, his pulse racing. It was changed, all right. No doubt about it.

"What's the matter, Ed?" Tom asked. The staff watched him curiously, pausing in their work.

Ed said nothing. He advanced slowly into the inner office. The office had been *gone over*. He could tell. Things had been altered. Rearranged. Nothing obvious-nothing he could put his finger on. But he could tell.

Joe Kent greeted him uneasily. "What's the matter, Ed? You look like a wild dog. Is something —?"

Ed studied Joe. He was different. Not the same. What was it?

Joe's face. It was a little fuller. His shirt was blue-striped. Joe never wore blue stripes. Ed examined Joe's desk. He saw papers and accounts. The desk-it was too far to the right. And it was bigger. It wasn't the same desk.

The picture on the wall. It wasn't the same. It was a different picture entirely. And the things on top of the file cabinet-some were new, others were gone.

He looked back through the door. Now that he thought about it, Miss Evans' hair was different, done a different way. And it was lighter.

In here, Mary, filing her nails, over by the window-she was taller, fuller. Her purse, lying on the desk in front of her —a red purse, red knit.

"You always...have that purse?" Ed demanded.

Mary glanced up. "What?"

"That purse. You always have that?"

Mary laughed. She smoothed her skirt coyly around her shapely thighs, her long lashes blinking modestly. "Why, Mr. Fletcher. What do you mean?"

Ed turned away. *He knew.* Even if she didn't. She had been redone-changed: her purse, her clothes, her figure, everything about her. None of them knew-but him. His mind spun dizzily. They were all changed. All of them were different. They had all been remolded, recast. Subtly-but it was there.

The wastebasket. It was smaller, not the same. The window shades-white, not ivory. The wall paper was not the same pattern. The lighting fixtures...

Endless, subtle changes.

Ed made his way back to the inner office. He lifted his hand and knocked on Douglas' door. "Come in."

Ed pushed the door open. Nathan Douglas looked up impatiently. "Mr. Douglas —" Ed began. He came into the room unsteadily-and stopped.

Douglas was not the same. Not at all. His whole office was changed: the rugs, the drapes. The desk was oak, not mahogany. And Douglas himself...

Douglas was younger, thinner. His hair, brown. His skin not so red. His face smoother. No wrinkles. Chin reshaped. Eyes green, not black. He was a different man. But still Douglas —a different Douglas. A different version!

"What is it?" Douglas demanded impatiently. "Oh, it's you, Fletcher. Where were you this morning?"

Ed backed out. Fast.

He slammed the door and hurried back through the inner office. Tom and Miss Evans glanced up, startled. Ed passed by them, grabbing the hall door open.

"Hey!" Tom called. "What —?"

Ed hurried down the hall. Terror leaped through him. He had to hurry. He had *seen.* There wasn't much time. He came to the elevator and stabbed the button.

No time.

He ran to the stairs and started down. He reached the second floor. His terror grew. It was a matter of seconds.

Seconds!

The public phone. Ed ran into the phone booth. He dragged the door shut after him. Wildly, he dropped a dime in the slot and dialed. He had to call the police. He held the receiver to his ear, his heart pounding.

Warn them. Changes. Somebody tampering with reality. Altering it. He had been right. The white-clad men...their equipment...going through the building.

"Hello!" Ed shouted hoarsely. There was no answer. No hum. Nothing.

Ed peered frantically out the door.

And he sagged, defeated. Slowly, he hung up the telephone receiver.

He was no longer on the second floor. The phone booth was rising, leaving the second floor behind, carrying him up, faster and faster. It rose floor by floor, moving silently, swiftly.

The phone booth passed through the ceiling of the building and out into the bright sunlight. It gained speed. The ground fell away below. Buildings and streets were getting smaller each moment. Tiny specks hurried along, far below, cars and people, dwindling rapidly.

Clouds drifted between him and the earth. Ed shut his eyes, dizzy with fright. He held on desperately to the door handles of the phone booth.

Faster and faster the phone booth climbed. The earth was rapidly being left behind, far below. Ed peered up wildly. *Where?* Where was he going? Where was it taking him?

He stood gripping the door handles, waiting.

The Clerk nodded curtly. "That's him, all right. The element in question."

Ed Fletcher looked around him. He was in a huge chamber. The edges fell away into indistinct shadows. In front of him stood a man with notes and ledgers under his arm, peering at him through steel-rimmed glasses. He was a nervous little man, sharp-eyed, with celluloid collar, blue-serge suit, vest, watch chain. He wore black shiny shoes.

And beyond him —

An old man sat quietly, in an immense modern chair. He watched Fletcher calmly, his blue eyes mild and tired. A strange thrill shot through Fletcher. It was not fear. Rather it was a vibration, rattling his bones —a deep sense of awe, tinged with fascination.

"Where-what is this place?" he asked faintly. He was still dazed from his quick ascent.

"Don't ask questions!" the nervous little man snapped angrily, tapping his pencil against his ledgers. "You're here to answer, not ask."

The Old Man moved a little. He raised his hand. "I will speak to the element alone," he murmured. His voice was low. It vibrated and rumbled through the chamber. Again the wave of fascinated awe swept Ed.

"Alone?" The little fellow backed away, gathering his books and papers in his arms. "Of course." He glanced hostilely at Ed Fletcher. "I'm glad he's finally in custody. All the work and trouble just for —"

He disappeared through a door. The door closed softly behind him. Ed and the Old Man were alone.

"Please sit down," the Old Man said.

Ed found a seat. He sat down awkwardly, nervously. He got out his cigarettes and then put them away again.

"What's wrong?" the Old Man asked.

"I'm just beginning to understand."

"Understand what?"

"That I'm dead."

The Old Man smiled briefly. "Dead? No, you're not dead. You're...visiting. An unusual event, but necessitated by circumstances." He leaned toward Ed. "Mr. Fletcher, you have got yourself involved in something."

"Yeah," Ed agreed. "I wish I knew what it was. Or how it happened."

"It was not your fault. You're the victim of a clerical error. A mistake was made-not by you. But involving you."

"What mistake?" Ed rubbed his forehead wearily. "I —I got in on something. I saw *through*. I saw something I wasn't supposed to see."

The Old Man nodded. "That's right. You saw something you were not supposed to see-something few elements have been aware of, let alone witnessed."

"Elements?"

"An official term. Let it pass. A mistake was made, but we hope to rectify it. It is my hope that —"

"Those people," Ed interrupted. "Heaps of dry ash. And gray. Like they were dead. Only it was everything: the stairs and walls and floor. No color or life."

"That Sector had been temporarily de-energized. So the adjustment team could enter and effect changes."

"Changes." Ed nodded. "That's right. When I went back later, everything was alive again. But not the same. It was all different."

"The adjustment was complete by noon. The team finished its work and re-energized the Sector."

"I see," Ed muttered.

"You were supposed to have been in the Sector when the adjustment began. Because of an error you were not. You came into the Sector late-during the adjustment itself. You fled, and when you returned it was over. You saw, and you should not have seen. Instead of a witness you should have been part of the adjustment. Like the others, you should have undergone changes."

Sweat came out on Ed Fletcher's head. He wiped it away. His stomach turned over. Weakly, he cleared his throat. "I get the picture." His voice was almost inaudible. A chilling premonition moved through him. "I was supposed to be changed like the others. But I guess something went wrong."

"Something went wrong. An error occurred. And now a serious problem exists. You have seen these things. You know a great deal. And you are not coordinated with the new configuration."

"Gosh," Ed muttered. "Well, I won't tell anybody." Cold sweat poured off him. "You can count on that. I'm as good as changed."

"You have already told someone," the Old Man said coldly.

"Me?" Ed blinked. "Who?"

"Your wife."

Ed trembled. The color drained from his face, leaving it sickly white. "That's right. I did."

"Your wife knows." The Old Man's face twisted angrily. "A woman. Of all the things to tell —"

"I didn't know." Ed retreated, panic leaping through him. "But I know *now*. You can count on me. Consider me changed."

The ancient blue eyes bored keenly into him, peering far into his depths. "And you were going to call the police. You wanted to inform the authorities."

"But I didn't know *who* was doing the changing."

"Now you know. The natural process must be supplemented-adjusted here and there. Corrections must be made. We are fully licensed to make such corrections. Our adjustment teams perform vital work."

Ed plucked up a measure of courage. "This particular adjustment. Douglas. The office. What was it for? I'm sure it was some worthwhile purpose."

The Old Man waved his hand. Behind him in the shadows an immense map glowed into existence. Ed caught his breath. The edges of the map faded off in obscurity. He saw an infinite web of detailed sections, a network of squares and ruled lines. Each square was marked. Some glowed with a blue light. The lights altered constantly.

"The Sector Board," the Old Man said. He sighed wearily. "A staggering job. Sometimes we wonder how we can go on another period. But it must be done. For the good of all. For *your* good."

"The change. In our-our Sector."

"Your office deals in real estate. The old Douglas was a shrewd man, but rapidly becoming infirm. His physical health was waning. In a few days Douglas will be offered a chance to purchase a large unimproved forest area in western Canada. It will require most of his assets. The older, less virile Douglas would have hesitated. It is imperative he not hesitate. He must purchase the area and clear the land at once. Only a younger man —a younger Douglas-would undertake this.

"When the land is cleared, certain anthropological remains will be discovered. They have already been placed there. Douglas will lease his land to the Canadian Government for scientific study. The remains found there will cause international excitement in learned circles.

"A chain of events will be set in motion. Men from numerous countries will come to Canada to examine the remains. Soviet, Polish, and Czech scientists will make the journey.

"The chain of events will draw these scientists together for the first time in years. National research will be temporarily forgotten in the excitement of these non-national discoveries. One of the leading Soviet scientists will make friends with a Belgian scientist. Before they depart they will agree to correspond-without the knowledge of their governments, of course.

"The circle will widen. Other scientists on both sides will be drawn in. A society will be founded. More and more educated men will transfer an increasing amount of time to this international society. Purely national research will suffer a slight but extremely critical eclipse. The war tension will somewhat wane.

"This alteration is vital. And it is dependent on the purchase and clearing of the section of wilderness in Canada. The old Douglas would not have dared take the risk. But the altered Douglas, and his altered, more youthful staff, will pursue this work with wholehearted enthusiasm. And from this, the vital chain of widening events will come about. The beneficiaries will be *you*. Our methods may seem strange and indirect. Even incomprehensible. But I assure you we know what we're doing."

"I know that now," Ed said.

"So you do. You know a great deal. Much too much. No element should possess such knowledge. I should perhaps call an adjustment team in here..."

A picture formed in Ed's mind: swirling gray clouds, gray men and women. He shuddered. "Look," he croaked. "I'll do anything. Anything at all. Only don't de-energize me." Sweat ran down his face. "Okay?"

The Old Man pondered. "Perhaps some alternative could be found. There is another possibility..."

"What?" Ed asked eagerly. "What is it?"

The Old Man spoke slowly, thoughtfully. "If I allow you to return, you will swear never to speak of the matter? Will you swear not to reveal to anyone the things you saw? The things you know?"

"Sure!" Ed gasped eagerly, blinding relief flooding over him. "I swear!"

"Your wife. She must know nothing more. She must think it was only a passing psychological fit-retreat from reality."

"She thinks that already."

"She must continue to."

Ed set his jaw firmly. "I'll see that she continues to think it was a mental aberration. She'll never know what really happened."

"You are certain you can keep the truth from her?"

"Sure," Ed said confidently. "I know I can."

"All right." The Old Man nodded slowly. "I will send you back. But you must tell no one." He swelled visibly. "Remember: you will eventually come back to me-everyone does, in the end-and your fate will not be enviable."

"I won't tell her," Ed said, sweating. "I promise. You have my word on that. I can handle Ruth. Don't give it a second thought."

Ed arrived home at sunset.

He blinked, dazed from the rapid descent. For a moment he stood on the pavement, regaining his balance and catching his breath. Then he walked quickly up the path.

He pushed the door open and entered the little green stucco house.

"Ed!" Ruth came flying, face distorted with tears. She threw her arms around him, hugging him tight. "Where the hell have you been?"

"Been?" Ed murmured. "At the office, of course."

Ruth pulled back abruptly. "No, you haven't."

Vague tendrils of alarm plucked at Ed. "Of course I have. Where else —?"

"I called Douglas about three. He said you left. You walked out, practically as soon as I turned my back. Eddie —"

Ed patted her nervously. "Take it easy, honey." He began unbuttoning his coat. "Everything's okay. Understand? Things are perfectly all right."

Ruth sat down on the arm of the couch. She blew her nose, dabbing at her eyes. "If you knew how much I've worried." She put her handkerchief away and folded her arms. "I want to know where you were."

Uneasily, Ed hung his coat in the closet. He came over and kissed her. Her lips were ice cold. "I'll tell you all about it. But what do you say we have something to eat? I'm starved."

Ruth studied him intently. She got down from the arm of the couch. "I'll change and fix dinner."

She hurried into the bedroom and slipped off her shoes and nylons. Ed followed her. "I didn't mean to worry you," he said carefully. "After you left me today I realized you were right."

"Oh?" Ruth unfastened her blouse and skirt, arranging them over a hanger. "Right about what?"

"About me." He manufactured a grin and made it glow across his face. "About...what happened."

Ruth hung her slip over the hanger. She studied her husband intently as she struggled into her tight-fitting jeans. "Go on."

The moment had come. It was now or never. Ed Fletcher braced himself and chose his words carefully. "I realized," he stated, "that the whole darn thing was in my mind. You were right, Ruth. Completely right. And I even realize what caused it."

Ruth rolled her cotton T-shirt down and tucked it in her jeans. "What was the cause?"

"Overwork."

"Overwork?"

"I need a vacation. I haven't had a vacation in years. My mind isn't on my job. I've been daydreaming." He said it firmly, but his heart was in his mouth. "I need to get away. To the mountains. Bass fishing. Or —" He searched his mind frantically. "Or —"

Ruth came toward him ominously. "Ed!" she said sharply. "Look at me!"

"What's the matter?" Panic shot through him. "Why are you looking at me like that?"

"Where were you this afternoon?"

Ed's grin faded. "I told you. I went for a walk. Didn't I tell you? A walk. To think things over."

"Don't lie to me, Eddie Fletcher! I can tell when you're lying!" Fresh tears welled up in Ruth's eyes. Her breasts rose and fell excitedly under her cotton shirt. "Admit it! You didn't go for a walk!"

Ed stammered weakly. Sweat poured off him. He sagged helplessly against the door. "What do you mean?"

Ruth's black eyes flashed with anger. "Come on! I want to know where you were! Tell me! I have a right to know. What really happened?"

Ed retreated in terror, his resolve melting like wax. It was going all wrong. "Honest. I went out for a —"

"Tell me!" Ruth's sharp fingernails dug into his arm. "I want to know where you were-and who you were with!"

Ed opened his mouth. He tried to grin, but his face failed to respond. "I don't know what you mean."

"You know what I mean. Who were you with? Where did you go? Tell me! I'll find out, sooner or later."

There was no way out. He was licked-and he knew it. He couldn't keep it from her. Desperately he stalled, praying for time. If he could only distract her, get her mind on something else. If she would only let up, even for a second. He could invent something —a better story. Time-he needed more time. "Ruth, you've got to —"

Suddenly there was a sound: the bark of a dog, echoing through the dark house.

Ruth let go, cocking her head alertly. "That was Dobbie. I think somebody's coming."

The doorbell rang.

"You stay here. I'll be right back." Ruth ran out of the room, to the front door. "Darn it." She pulled the front door open.

"Good evening!" The young man stepped quickly inside, loaded down with objects, grinning broadly at Ruth. "I'm from the Sweep-Rite Vacuum Cleaner Company."

Ruth scowled impatiently. "Really, we're about to sit down at the table."

"Oh, this will only take a moment." The young man set down the vacuum cleaner and its attachments with a metallic crash. Rapidly, he unrolled a long illustrated banner, showing the vacuum cleaner in action. "Now, if you'll just hold this while I plug in the cleaner —"

He bustled happily about, unplugging the TV set, plugging in the cleaner, pushing the chairs out of his way.

"I'll show you the drape scraper first." He attached a hose and nozzle to the big gleaming tank. "Now, if you'll just sit down I'll demonstrate each of these easy-to-use attachments." His happy voice rose over the roar of the cleaner. "You'll notice —"

Ed Fletcher sat down on the bed. He groped in his pocket until he found his cigarettes. Shakily he lit one and leaned back against the wall, weak with relief.

He gazed up, a look of gratitude on his face. "Thanks," he said softly. "I think we'll make it-after all. Thanks a lot."

The Defenders

Taylor sat back in his chair reading the morning newspaper. The warm kitchen and the smell of coffee blended with the comfort of not having to go to work. This was his Rest Period, the first for a long time, and he was glad of it. He folded the second section back, sighing with contentment.

"What is it?" Mary said, from the stove.

"They pasted Moscow again last night." Taylor nodded his head in approval. "Gave it a real pounding. One of those R-H bombs. It's about time."

He nodded again, feeling the full comfort of the kitchen, the presence of his plump, attractive wife, the breakfast dishes and coffee. This was relaxation. And the war news was good, good and satisfying. He could feel a justifiable glow at the news, a sense of pride and personal accomplishment. After all, he was an integral part of the war program, not just another factory worker lugging a cart of scrap, but a technician, one of those who designed and planned the nerve-trunk of the war.

"It says they have the new subs almost perfected. Wait until they get *those* going." He smacked his lips with anticipation. "When they start shelling from underwater, the Soviets are sure going to be surprised."

"They're doing a wonderful job," Mary agreed vaguely. "Do you know what we saw today? Our team is getting a leady to show to the school children. I saw the leady, but only for a moment. It's good for the children to see what their contributions are going for, don't you think?"

She looked around at him.

"A leady," Taylor murmured. He put the newspaper slowly down. "Well, make sure it's decontaminated properly. We don't want to take any chances."

"Oh, they always bathe them when they're brought down from the surface," Mary said. "They wouldn't think of letting them down without the bath. Would they?" She hesitated, thinking back. "Don, you know, it makes me remember —"

He nodded. "I know."

* * * * *

He knew what she was thinking. Once in the very first weeks of the war, before everyone had been evacuated from the surface, they had seen a hospital train discharging the wounded, people who had been showered with sleet. He remembered the way they had looked, the expression on their faces, or as much of their faces as was left. It had not been a pleasant sight.

There had been a lot of that at first, in the early days before the transfer to undersurface was complete. There had been a lot, and it hadn't been very difficult to come across it.

Taylor looked up at his wife. She was thinking too much about it, the last few months. They all were.

"Forget it," he said. "It's all in the past. There isn't anybody up there now but the leadys, and they don't mind."

"But just the same, I hope they're careful when they let one of them down here. If one were still hot —"

He laughed, pushing himself away from the table. "Forget it. This is a wonderful moment; I'll be home for the next two shifts. Nothing to do but sit around and take things easy. Maybe we can take in a show. Okay?"

"A show? Do we have to? I don't like to look at all the destruction, the ruins. Sometimes I see some place I remember, like San Francisco. They showed a shot of San Francisco, the bridge broken and fallen in the water, and I got upset. I don't like to watch."

"But don't you want to know what's going on? No human beings are getting hurt, you know."

"But it's so awful!" Her face was set and strained. "Please, no, Don."

Don Taylor picked up his newspaper sullenly. "All right, but there isn't a hell of a lot else to do. And don't forget, *their* cities are getting it even worse."

She nodded. Taylor turned the rough, thin sheets of newspaper. His good mood had soured on him. Why did she have to fret all the time? They were pretty well off, as things went. You couldn't expect to have everything perfect, living undersurface, with an artificial sun and artificial food. Naturally it was a strain, not seeing the sky or being able to go any place or see anything other than metal walls, great roaring factories, the plant-yards, barracks. But it was better than being on surface. And some day it would end and they could return. Nobody *wanted* to live this way, but it was necessary.

He turned the page angrily and the poor paper ripped. Damn it, the paper was getting worse quality all the time, bad print, yellow tint —

Well, they needed everything for the war program. He ought to know that. Wasn't he one of the planners?

He excused himself and went into the other room. The bed was still unmade. They had better get it in shape before the seventh hour inspection. There was a one unit fine —

The vidphone rang. He halted. Who would it be? He went over and clicked it on.

"Taylor?" the face said, forming into place. It was an old face, gray and grim. "This is Moss. I'm sorry to bother you during Rest Period, but this thing has come up." He rattled papers. "I want you to hurry over here."

Taylor stiffened. "What is it? There's no chance it could wait?" The calm gray eyes were studying him, expressionless, unjudging. "If you want me to come down to the lab," Taylor grumbled, "I suppose I can. I'll get my uniform —"

"No. Come as you are. And not to the lab. Meet me at second stage as soon as possible. It'll take you about a half hour, using the fast car up. I'll see you there."

The picture broke and Moss disappeared.

* * * * *

"What was it?" Mary said, at the door.

"Moss. He wants me for something."

"I knew this would happen."

"Well, you didn't want to do anything, anyhow. What does it matter?" His voice was bitter. "It's all the same, every day. I'll bring you back something. I'm going up to second stage. Maybe I'll be close enough to the surface to —"

"Don't! Don't bring me anything! Not from the surface!"

"All right, I won't. But of all the irrational nonsense —"

She watched him put on his boots without answering.

* * * * *

Moss nodded and Taylor fell in step with him, as the older man strode along. A series of loads were going up to the surface, blind cars clanking like ore-trucks up the ramp, disappearing through the stage trap above them. Taylor watched the cars, heavy with tubular machinery of some sort, weapons new to him. Workers were everywhere, in the dark gray uniforms of the labor corps, loading, lifting, shouting back and forth. The stage was deafening with noise.

"We'll go up a way," Moss said, "where we can talk. This is no place to give you details."

They took an escalator up. The commercial lift fell behind them, and with it most of the crashing and booming. Soon they emerged on an observation platform, suspended on the side of the Tube, the vast tunnel leading to the surface, not more than half a mile above them now.

"My God!" Taylor said, looking down the Tube involuntarily. "It's a long way down."

Moss laughed. "Don't look."

They opened a door and entered an office. Behind the desk, an officer was sitting, an officer of Internal Security. He looked up.

"I'll be right with you, Moss." He gazed at Taylor studying him. "You're a little ahead of time."

"This is Commander Franks," Moss said to Taylor. "He was the first to make the discovery. I was notified last night." He tapped a parcel he carried. "I was let in because of this."

Franks frowned at him and stood up. "We're going up to first stage. We can discuss it there."

"First stage?" Taylor repeated nervously. The three of them went down a side passage to a small lift. "I've never been up there. Is it all right? It's not radioactive, is it?"

"You're like everyone else," Franks said. "Old women afraid of burglars. No radiation leaks down to first stage. There's lead and rock, and what comes down the Tube is bathed."

"What's the nature of the problem?" Taylor asked. "I'd like to know something about it."

"In a moment."

They entered the lift and ascended. When they stepped out, they were in a hall of soldiers, weapons and uniforms everywhere. Taylor blinked in surprise. So this was first stage, the closest undersurface level to the top! After this stage there was only rock, lead and rock, and the great tubes leading up like the burrows of earthworms. Lead and rock, and above that, where the tubes opened, the great expanse that no living being had seen for eight years, the vast, endless ruin that had once been Man's home, the place where he had lived, eight years ago.

Now the surface was a lethal desert of slag and rolling clouds. Endless clouds drifted back and forth, blotting out the red Sun. Occasionally something metallic stirred, moving through the remains of a city, threading its way across the tortured terrain of the countryside. A leady, a surface robot, immune to radiation, constructed with feverish haste in the last months before the cold war became literally hot.

Leadys, crawling along the ground, moving over the oceans or through the skies in slender, blackened craft, creatures that could exist where no *life* could remain, metal and plastic figures that waged a war Man had conceived, but which he could not fight himself. Human beings had invented war, invented and manufactured the weapons, even invented the players, the fighters, the actors of the war. But they themselves could not venture forth, could not wage it themselves. In all the world-in Russia, in Europe, America, Africa-no living human being remained. They were under the surface, in the deep shelters that had been carefully planned and built, even as the first bombs began to fall.

It was a brilliant idea and the only idea that could have worked. Up above, on the ruined, blasted surface of what had once been a living planet, the leady crawled and scurried, and fought Man's war. And undersurface, in the depths of the planet, human beings toiled endlessly to produce the weapons to continue the fight, month by month, year by year.

* * * * *

"First stage," Taylor said. A strange ache went through him. "Almost to the surface."

"But not quite," Moss said.

Franks led them through the soldiers, over to one side, near the lip of the Tube.

"In a few minutes, a lift will bring something down to us from the surface," he explained. "You see, Taylor, every once in a while Security examines and interrogates a surface leady, one that has been above for a time, to find out certain things. A vidcall is sent up and contact is made with a field headquarters. We need this direct interview; we can't depend on vidscreen contact alone. The leadys are doing a good job, but we want to make certain that everything is going the way we want it."

Franks faced Taylor and Moss and continued: "The lift will bring down a leady from the surface, one of the A-class leadys. There's an examination chamber in the next room, with a lead wall in the center, so the interviewing officers won't be exposed to radiation. We find this easier than bathing the leady. It is going right back up; it has a job to get back to.

"Two days ago, an A-class leady was brought down and interrogated. I conducted the session myself. We were interested in a new weapon the Soviets have been using, an automatic mine that pursues anything that moves. Military had sent instructions up that the mine be observed and reported in detail.

"This A-class leady was brought down with information. We learned a few facts from it, obtained the usual roll of film and reports, and then sent it back up. It was going out of the chamber, back to the lift, when a curious thing happened. At the time, I thought —"

Franks broke off. A red light was flashing.

"That down lift is coming." He nodded to some soldiers. "Let's enter the chamber. The leady will be along in a moment."

"An A-class leady," Taylor said. "I've seen them on the showscreens, making their reports."

"It's quite an experience," Moss said. "They're almost human."

* * * * *

They entered the chamber and seated themselves behind the lead wall. After a time, a signal was flashed, and Franks made a motion with his hands.

The door beyond the wall opened. Taylor peered through his view slot. He saw something advancing slowly, a slender metallic figure moving on a tread, its arm grips at rest by its sides. The figure halted and scanned the lead wall. It stood, waiting.

"We are interested in learning something," Franks said. "Before I question you, do you have anything to report on surface conditions?"

"No. The war continues." The leady's voice was automatic and toneless. "We are a little short of fast pursuit craft, the single-seat type. We could use also some —"

"That has all been noted. What I want to ask you is this. Our contact with you has been through vidscreen only. We must rely on indirect evidence, since none of us goes above. We can only infer what is going on. We never see anything ourselves. We have to take it all secondhand. Some top leaders are beginning to think there's too much room for error."

"Error?" the leady asked. "In what way? Our reports are checked carefully before they're sent down. We maintain constant contact with you; everything of value is reported. Any new weapons which the enemy is seen to employ —"

"I realize that," Franks grunted behind his peep slot. "But perhaps we should see it all for ourselves. Is it possible that there might be a large enough radiation-free area for a human party to ascend to the surface? If a few of us were to come up in lead-lined suits, would we be able to survive long enough to observe conditions and watch things?"

The machine hesitated before answering. "I doubt it. You can check air samples, of course, and decide for yourselves. But in the eight years since you left, things have continually worsened. You cannot have any real idea of conditions up there. It has become difficult for any moving object to survive for long. There are many kinds of projectiles sensitive to movement. The new mine not only reacts to motion, but continues to pursue the object indefinitely, until it finally reaches it. And the radiation is everywhere."

"I see." Franks turned to Moss, his eyes narrowed oddly. "Well, that was what I wanted to know. You may go."

The machine moved back toward its exit. It paused. "Each month the amount of lethal particles in the atmosphere increases. The tempo of the war is gradually —"

"I understand." Franks rose. He held out his hand and Moss passed him the package. "One thing before you leave. I want you to examine a new type of metal shield material. I'll pass you a sample with the tong."

Franks put the package in the toothed grip and revolved the tong so that he held the other end. The package swung down to the leady, which took it. They watched it unwrap the package and take the metal plate in its hands. The leady turned the metal over and over.

Suddenly it became rigid.

"All right," Franks said.

He put his shoulder against the wall and a section slid aside. Taylor gasped-Franks and Moss were hurrying up to the leady!

"Good God!" Taylor said. "But it's radioactive!"

* * * * *

The leady stood unmoving, still holding the metal. Soldiers appeared in the chamber. They surrounded the leady and ran a counter across it carefully.

"Okay, sir," one of them said to Franks. "It's as cold as a long winter evening."

"Good. I was sure, but I didn't want to take any chances."

"You see," Moss said to Taylor, "this leady isn't hot at all. Yet it came directly from the surface, without even being bathed."

"But what does it mean?" Taylor asked blankly.

"It may be an accident," Franks said. "There's always the possibility that a given object might escape being exposed above. But this is the second time it's happened that we know of. There may be others."

"The second time?"

"The previous interview was when we noticed it. The leady was not hot. It was cold, too, like this one."

Moss took back the metal plate from the leady's hands. He pressed the surface carefully and returned it to the stiff, unprotesting fingers.

"We shorted it out with this, so we could get close enough for a thorough check. It'll come back on in a second now. We had better get behind the wall again."

They walked back and the lead wall swung closed behind them. The soldiers left the chamber.

"Two periods from now," Franks said softly, "an initial investigating party will be ready to go surface-side. We're going up the Tube in suits, up to the top-the first human party to leave undersurface in eight years."

"It may mean nothing," Moss said, "but I doubt it. Something's going on, something strange. The leady told us no life could exist above without being roasted. The story doesn't fit."

Taylor nodded. He stared through the peep slot at the immobile metal figure. Already the leady was beginning to stir. It was bent in several places, dented and twisted, and its finish was blackened and charred. It was a leady that had been up there a long time; it had seen war and destruction, ruin so vast that no human being could imagine the extent. It had crawled and slunk in a world of radiation and death, a world where no life could exist.

And Taylor had touched it!

"You're going with us," Franks said suddenly. "I want you along. I think the three of us will go."

* * * * *

Mary faced him with a sick and frightened expression. "I know it. You're going to the surface. Aren't you?"

She followed him into the kitchen. Taylor sat down, looking away from her.

"It's a classified project," he evaded. "I can't tell you anything about it."

"You don't have to tell me. I know. I knew it the moment you came in. There was something on your face, something I haven't seen there for a long, long time. It was an old look."

She came toward him. "But how can they send you to the surface?" She took his face in her shaking hands, making him look at her. There was a strange hunger in her eyes. "Nobody can live up there. Look, look at this!"

She grabbed up a newspaper and held it in front of him.

"Look at this photograph. America, Europe, Asia, Africa-nothing but ruins. We've seen it every day on the showscreens. All destroyed, poisoned. And they're sending you up. Why? No living thing can get by up there, not even a weed, or grass. They've wrecked the surface, haven't they? *Haven't they?*"

Taylor stood up. "It's an order. I know nothing about it. I was told to report to join a scout party. That's all I know."

He stood for a long time, staring ahead. Slowly, he reached for the newspaper and held it up to the light.

"It looks real," he murmured. "Ruins, deadness, slag. It's convincing. All the reports, photographs, films, even air samples. Yet we haven't seen it for ourselves, not after the first months..."

"What are you talking about?"

"Nothing." He put the paper down. "I'm leaving early after the next Sleep Period. Let's turn in."

Mary turned away, her face hard and harsh. "Do what you want. We might just as well all go up and get killed at once, instead of dying slowly down here, like vermin in the ground."

He had not realized how resentful she was. Were they all like that? How about the workers toiling in the factories, day and night, endlessly? The pale, stooped men and women, plodding back and forth to work, blinking in the colorless light, eating synthetics —

"You shouldn't be so bitter," he said.

Mary smiled a little. "I'm bitter because I know you'll never come back." She turned away. "I'll never see you again, once you go up there."

He was shocked. "What? How can you say a thing like that?"

She did not answer.

* * * * *

He awakened with the public newscaster screeching in his ears, shouting outside the building.

"Special news bulletin! Surface forces report enormous Soviet attack with new weapons! Retreat of key groups! All work units report to factories at once!"

Taylor blinked, rubbing his eyes. He jumped out of bed and hurried to the vidphone. A moment later he was put through to Moss.

"Listen," he said. "What about this new attack? Is the project off?" He could see Moss's desk, covered with reports and papers.

"No," Moss said. "We're going right ahead. Get over here at once."

"But —"

"Don't argue with me." Moss held up a handful of surface bulletins, crumpling them savagely. "This is a fake. Come on!" He broke off.

Taylor dressed furiously, his mind in a daze.

Half an hour later, he leaped from a fast car and hurried up the stairs into the Synthetics Building. The corridors were full of men and women rushing in every direction. He entered Moss's office.

"There you are," Moss said, getting up immediately. "Franks is waiting for us at the outgoing station."

They went in a Security Car, the siren screaming. Workers scattered out of their way.

"What about the attack?" Taylor asked.

Moss braced his shoulders. "We're certain that we've forced their hand. We've brought the issue to a head."

They pulled up at the station link of the Tube and leaped out. A moment later they were moving up at high speed toward the first stage.

They emerged into a bewildering scene of activity. Soldiers were fastening on lead suits, talking excitedly to each other, shouting back and forth. Guns were being given out, instructions passed.

Taylor studied one of the soldiers. He was armed with the dreaded Bender pistol, the new snub-nosed hand weapon that was just beginning to come from the assembly line. Some of the soldiers looked a little frightened.

"I hope we're not making a mistake," Moss said, noticing his gaze.

Franks came toward them. "Here's the program. The three of us are going up first, alone. The soldiers will follow in fifteen minutes."

"What are we going to tell the leadys?" Taylor worriedly asked. "We'll have to tell them something."

"We want to observe the new Soviet attack." Franks smiled ironically. "Since it seems to be so serious, we should be there in person to witness it."

"And then what?" Taylor said.

"That'll be up to them. Let's go."

* * * * *

In a small car, they went swiftly up the Tube, carried by anti-grav beams from below. Taylor glanced down from time to time. It was a long way back, and getting longer each moment. He sweated nervously inside his suit, gripping his Bender pistol with inexpert fingers.

Why had they chosen him? Chance, pure chance. Moss had asked him to come along as a Department member. Then Franks had picked him out on the spur of the moment. And now they were rushing toward the surface, faster and faster.

A deep fear, instilled in him for eight years, throbbed in his mind. Radiation, certain death, a world blasted and lethal —

Up and up the car went. Taylor gripped the sides and closed his eyes. Each moment they were closer, the first living creatures to go above the first stage, up the Tube past the lead and rock, up to the surface. The phobic horror shook him in waves. It was death; they all knew that. Hadn't they seen it in the films a thousand times? The cities, the sleet coming down, the rolling clouds —

"It won't be much longer," Franks said. "We're almost there. The surface tower is not expecting us. I gave orders that no signal was to be sent."

The car shot up, rushing furiously. Taylor's head spun; he hung on, his eyes shut. Up and up....

The car stopped. He opened his eyes.

They were in a vast room, fluorescent-lit, a cavern filled with equipment and machinery, endless mounds of material piled in row after row. Among the stacks, leadys were working silently, pushing trucks and handcarts.

"Leadys," Moss said. His face was pale. "Then we're really on the surface."

The leadys were going back and forth with equipment moving the vast stores of guns and spare parts, ammunition and supplies that had been brought to the surface. And this was the receiving station for only one Tube; there were many others, scattered throughout the continent.

Taylor looked nervously around him. They were really there, above ground, on the surface. This was where the war was.

"Come on," Franks said. "A B-class guard is coming our way."

* * * * *

They stepped out of the car. A leady was approaching them rapidly. It coasted up in front of them and stopped, scanning them with its hand-weapon raised.

"This is Security," Franks said. "Have an A-class sent to me at once."

The leady hesitated. Other B-class guards were coming, scooting across the floor, alert and alarmed. Moss peered around.

"Obey!" Franks said in a loud, commanding voice. "You've been ordered!"

The leady moved uncertainly away from them. At the end of the building, a door slid back. Two A-class leadys appeared, coming slowly toward them. Each had a green stripe across its front.

"From the Surface Council," Franks whispered tensely. "This is above ground, all right. Get set."

The two leadys approached warily. Without speaking, they stopped close by the men, looking them up and down.

"I'm Franks of Security. We came from undersurface in order to —"

"This in incredible," one of the leadys interrupted him coldly. "You know you can't live up here. The whole surface is lethal to you. You can't possibly remain on the surface."

"These suits will protect us," Franks said. "In any case, it's not your responsibility. What I want is an immediate Council meeting so I can acquaint myself with conditions, with the situation here. Can that be arranged?"

"You human beings can't survive up here. And the new Soviet attack is directed at this area. It is in considerable danger."

"We know that. Please assemble the Council." Franks looked around him at the vast room, lit by recessed lamps in the ceiling. An uncertain quality came into his voice. "Is it night or day right now?"

"Night," one of the A-class leadys said, after a pause. "Dawn is coming in about two hours."

Franks nodded. "We'll remain at least two hours, then. As a concession to our sentimentality, would you please show us some place where we can observe the Sun as it comes up? We would appreciate it."

A stir went through the leadys.

"It is an unpleasant sight," one of the leadys said. "You've seen the photographs; you know what you'll witness. Clouds of drifting particles blot out the light, slag heaps are everywhere, the whole land is destroyed. For you it will be a staggering sight, much worse than pictures and film can convey."

"However it may be, we'll stay long enough to see it. Will you give the order to the Council?"

* * * * *

"Come this way." Reluctantly, the two leadys coasted toward the wall of the warehouse. The three men trudged after them, their heavy shoes ringing against the concrete. At the wall, the two leadys paused.

"This is the entrance to the Council Chamber. There are windows in the Chamber Room, but it is still dark outside, of course. You'll see nothing right now, but in two hours —"

"Open the door," Franks said.

The door slid back. They went slowly inside. The room was small, a neat room with a round table in the center, chairs ringing it. The three of them sat down silently, and the two leadys followed after them, taking their places.

"The other Council Members are on their way. They have already been notified and are coming as quickly as they can. Again I urge you to go back down." The leady surveyed the three human beings. "There is no way you can meet the conditions up here. Even we survive with some trouble, ourselves. How can you expect to do it?"

The leader approached Franks.

"This astonishes and perplexes us," it said. "Of course we must do what you tell us, but allow me to point out that if you remain here —"

"We know," Franks said impatiently. "However, we intend to remain, at least until sunrise."

"If you insist."

There was silence. The leadys seemed to be conferring with each other, although the three men heard no sound.

"For your own good," the leader said at last, "you must go back down. We have discussed this, and it seems to us that you are doing the wrong thing for your own good."

"We are human beings," Franks said sharply. "Don't you understand? We're men, not machines."

"That is precisely why you must go back. This room is radioactive; all surface areas are. We calculate that your suits will not protect you for over fifty more minutes. Therefore —"

The leadys moved abruptly toward the men, wheeling in a circle, forming a solid row. The men stood up, Taylor reaching awkwardly for his weapon, his fingers numb and stupid. The men stood facing the silent metal figures.

"We must insist," the leader said, its voice without emotion. "We must take you back to the Tube and send you down on the next car. I am sorry, but it is necessary."

"What'll we do?" Moss said nervously to Franks. He touched his gun. "Shall we blast them?"

Franks shook his head. "All right," he said to the leader. "We'll go back."

* * * * *

He moved toward the door, motioning Taylor and Moss to follow him. They looked at him in surprise, but they came with him. The leadys followed them out into the great warehouse. Slowly they moved toward the Tube entrance, none of them speaking.

At the lip, Franks turned. "We are going back because we have no choice. There are three of us and about a dozen of you. However, if —"

"Here comes the car," Taylor said.

There was a grating sound from the Tube. D-class leadys moved toward the edge to receive it.

"I am sorry," the leader said, "but it is for your protection. We are watching over you, literally. You must stay below and let us conduct the war. In a sense, it has come to be *our* war. We must fight it as we see fit."

The car rose to the surface.

Twelve soldiers, armed with Bender pistols, stepped from it and surrounded the three men. Moss breathed a sigh of relief. "Well, this does change things. It came off just right."

The leader moved back, away from the soldiers. It studied them intently, glancing from one to the next, apparently trying to make up its mind. At last it made a sign to the other leadys. They coasted aside and a corridor was opened up toward the warehouse.

"Even now," the leader said, "we could send you back by force. But it is evident that this is not really an observation party at all. These soldiers show that you have much more in mind; this was all carefully prepared."

"Very carefully," Franks said.

They closed in.

"How much more, we can only guess. I must admit that we were taken unprepared. We failed utterly to meet the situation. Now force would be absurd, because neither side can afford to injure the other; we, because of the restrictions placed on us regarding human life, you because the war demands —"

The soldiers fired, quick and in fright. Moss dropped to one knee, firing up. The leader dissolved in a cloud of particles. On all sides D- and B-class leadys were rushing up, some with weapons, some with metal slats. The room was in confusion. Off in the distance a siren was screaming. Franks and Taylor were cut off from the others, separated from the soldiers by a wall of metal bodies.

"They can't fire back," Franks said calmly. "This is another bluff. They've tried to bluff us all the way." He fired into the face of a leady. The leady dissolved. "They can only try to frighten us. Remember that."

*****

They went on firing and leady after leady vanished. The room reeked with the smell of burning metal, the stink of fused plastic and steel. Taylor had been knocked down. He was struggling to find his gun, reaching wildly among metal legs, groping frantically to find it. His fingers strained, a handle swam in front of him. Suddenly something came down on his arm, a metal foot. He cried out.

Then it was over. The leadys were moving away, gathering together off to one side. Only four of the Surface Council remained. The others were radioactive particles in the air. D-class leadys were already restoring order, gathering up partly destroyed metal figures and bits and removing them.

Franks breathed a shuddering sigh.

"All right," he said. "You can take us back to the windows. It won't be long now."

The leadys separated, and the human group, Moss and Franks and Taylor and the soldiers, walked slowly across the room, toward the door. They entered the Council Chamber. Already a faint touch of gray mitigated the blackness of the windows.

"Take us outside," Franks said impatiently. "We'll see it directly, not in here."

A door slid open. A chill blast of cold morning air rushed in, chilling them even through their lead suits. The men glanced at each other uneasily.

"Come on," Franks said. "Outside."

He walked out through the door, the others following him.

They were on a hill, overlooking the vast bowl of a valley. Dimly, against the graying sky, the outline of mountains were forming, becoming tangible.

"It'll be bright enough to see in a few minutes," Moss said. He shuddered as a chilling wind caught him and moved around him. "It's worth it, really worth it, to see this again after eight years. Even if it's the last thing we see —"

"Watch," Franks snapped.

They obeyed, silent and subdued. The sky was clearing, brightening each moment. Some place far off, echoing across the valley, a rooster crowed.

"A chicken!" Taylor murmured. "Did you hear?"

Behind them, the leadys had come out and were standing silently, watching, too. The gray sky turned to white and the hills appeared more clearly. Light spread across the valley floor, moving toward them.

"God in heaven!" Franks exclaimed.

Trees, trees and forests. A valley of plants and trees, with a few roads winding among them. Farmhouses. A windmill. A barn, far down below them.

"Look!" Moss whispered.

Color came into the sky. The Sun was approaching. Birds began to sing. Not far from where they stood, the leaves of a tree danced in the wind.

Franks turned to the row of leadys behind them.

"Eight years. We were tricked. There was no war. As soon as we left the surface —"

"Yes," an A-class leady admitted. "As soon as you left, the war ceased. You're right, it was a hoax. You worked hard undersurface, sending up guns and weapons, and we destroyed them as fast as they came up."

"But why?" Taylor asked, dazed. He stared down at the vast valley below. "Why?"

*****

"You created us," the leady said, "to pursue the war for you, while you human beings went below the ground in order to survive. But before we could continue the war, it was necessary to analyze it to determine what its purpose was. We did this, and we found that it had no purpose, except, perhaps, in terms of human needs. Even this was questionable.

"We investigated further. We found that human cultures pass through phases, each culture in its own time. As the culture ages and begins to lose its objectives, conflict arises within it between those who wish to cast it off and set up a new culture-pattern, and those who wish to retain the old with as little change as possible.

"At this point, a great danger appears. The conflict within threatens to engulf the society in self-war, group against group. The vital traditions may be lost-not merely altered or reformed, but completely destroyed in this period of chaos and anarchy. We have found many such examples in the history of mankind.

"It is necessary for this hatred within the culture to be directed outward, toward an external group, so that the culture itself may survive its crisis. War is the result. War, to a logical mind, is absurd. But in terms of human needs, it plays a vital role. And it will continue to until Man has grown up enough so that no hatred lies within him."

Taylor was listening intently. "Do you think this time will come?"

"Of course. It has almost arrived now. This is the last war. Man is *almost* united into one final culture —a world culture. At this point he stands continent against continent, one half of the world against the other half. Only a single step remains, the jump to a unified culture. Man has climbed slowly upward, tending always toward unification of his culture. It will not be long —

"But it has not come yet, and so the war had to go on, to satisfy the last violent surge of hatred that Man felt. Eight years have passed since the war began. In these eight years, we have observed and noted important changes going on in the minds of men. Fatigue and disinterest, we have seen, are gradually taking the place of hatred and fear. The hatred is being exhausted gradually, over a period of time. But for the present, the hoax must go on, at least for a while longer. You are not ready to learn the truth. You would want to continue the war."

"But how did you manage it?" Moss asked. "All the photographs, the samples, the damaged equipment —"

"Come over here." The leady directed them toward a long, low building. "Work goes on constantly, whole staffs laboring to maintain a coherent and convincing picture of a global war."

* * * * *

They entered the building. Leadys were working everywhere, poring over tables and desks.

"Examine this project here," the A-class leady said. Two leadys were carefully photographing something, an elaborate model on a table top. "It is a good example."

The men grouped around, trying to see. It was a model of a ruined city.

Taylor studied it in silence for a long time. At last he looked up.

"It's San Francisco," he said in a low voice. "This is a model of San Francisco, destroyed. I saw this on the vidscreen, piped down to us. The bridges were hit —"

"Yes, notice the bridges." The leady traced the ruined span with his metal finger, a tiny spider-web, almost invisible. "You have no doubt seen photographs of this many times, and of the other tables in this building.

"San Francisco itself is completely intact. We restored it soon after you left, rebuilding the parts that had been damaged at the start of the war. The work of manufacturing news goes on all the time in this particular building. We are very careful to see that each part fits in with all the other parts. Much time and effort are devoted to it."

Franks touched one of the tiny model buildings, lying half in ruins. "So this is what you spend your time doing-making model cities and then blasting them."

"No, we do much more. We are caretakers, watching over the whole world. The owners have left for a time, and we must see that the cities are kept clean, that decay is prevented, that everything is kept oiled and in running condition. The gardens, the streets, the water mains, everything must be maintained as it was eight years ago, so that when the owners return, they will not be displeased. We want to be sure that they will be completely satisfied."

Franks tapped Moss on the arm.

"Come over here," he said in a low voice. "I want to talk to you."

He led Moss and Taylor out of the building, away from the leadys, outside on the hillside. The soldiers followed them. The Sun was up and the sky was turning blue. The air smelled sweet and good, the smell of growing things.

Taylor removed his helmet and took a deep breath.

"I haven't smelled that smell for a long time," he said.

"Listen," Franks said, his voice low and hard. "We must get back down at once. There's a lot to get started on. All this can be turned to our advantage."

"What do you mean?" Moss asked.

"It's a certainty that the Soviets have been tricked, too, the same as us. But *we* have found out. That gives us an edge over them."

"I see." Moss nodded. "We know, but they don't. Their Surface Council has sold out, the same as ours. It works against them the same way. But if we could —"

"With a hundred top-level men, we could take over again, restore things as they should be! It would be easy!"

* * * * *

Moss touched him on the arm. An A-class leady was coming from the building toward them.

"We've seen enough," Franks said, raising his voice. "All this is very serious. It must be reported below and a study made to determine our policy."

The leady said nothing.

Franks waved to the soldiers. "Let's go." He started toward the warehouse.

Most of the soldiers had removed their helmets. Some of them had taken their lead suits off, too, and were relaxing comfortably in their cotton uniforms. They stared around them, down the hillside at the trees and bushes, the vast expanse of green, the mountains and the sky.

"Look at the Sun," one of them murmured.

"It sure is bright as hell," another said.

"We're going back down," Franks said. "Fall in by twos and follow us."

Reluctantly, the soldiers regrouped. The leadys watched without emotion as the men marched slowly back toward the warehouse. Franks and Moss and Taylor led them across the ground, glancing alertly at the leadys as they walked.

They entered the warehouse. D-class leadys were loading material and weapons on surface carts. Cranes and derricks were working busily everywhere. The work was done with efficiency, but without hurry or excitement.

The men stopped, watching. Leadys operating the little carts moved past them, signaling silently to each other. Guns and parts were being hoisted by magnetic cranes and lowered gently onto waiting carts.

"Come on," Franks said.

He turned toward the lip of the Tube. A row of D-class leadys was standing in front of it, immobile and silent. Franks stopped, moving back. He looked around. An A-class leady was coming toward him.

"Tell them to get out of the way," Franks said. He touched his gun. "You had better move them."

Time passed, an endless moment, without measure. The men stood, nervous and alert, watching the row of leadys in front of them.

"As you wish," the A-class leady said.

It signaled and the D-class leadys moved into life. They stepped slowly aside.

Moss breathed a sigh of relief.

"I'm glad that's over," he said to Franks. "Look at them all. Why don't they try to stop us? They must know what we're going to do."

Franks laughed. "Stop us? You saw what happened when they tried to stop us before. They can't; they're only machines. We built them so they can't lay hands on us, and they know that."

His voice trailed off.

The men stared at the Tube entrance. Around them the leadys watched, silent and impassive, their metal faces expressionless.

For a long time the men stood without moving. At last Taylor turned away.

"Good God," he said. He was numb, without feeling of any kind.

The Tube was gone. It was sealed shut, fused over. Only a dull surface of cooling metal greeted them.

The Tube had been closed.

* * * * *

Franks turned, his face pale and vacant.

The A-class leady shifted. "As you can see, the Tube has been shut. We were prepared for this. As soon as all of you were on the surface, the order was given. If you had gone back when we asked you, you would now be safely down below. We had to work quickly because it was such an immense operation."

"But why?" Moss demanded angrily.

"Because it is unthinkable that you should be allowed to resume the war. With all the Tubes sealed, it will be many months before forces from below can reach the surface, let alone organize a military program. By that time the cycle will have entered its last stages. You will not be so perturbed to find your world intact.

"We had hoped that you would be undersurface when the sealing occurred. Your presence here is a nuisance. When the Soviets broke through, we were able to accomplish their sealing without —"

"The Soviets? They broke through?"

"Several months ago, they came up unexpectedly to see why the war had not been won. We were forced to act with speed. At this moment they are desperately attempting to cut new Tubes to the surface, to resume the war. We have, however, been able to seal each new one as it appears."

The leady regarded the three men calmly.

"We're cut off," Moss said, trembling. "We can't get back. What'll we do?"

"How did you manage to seal the Tube so quickly?" Franks asked the leady. "We've been up here only two hours."

"Bombs are placed just above the first stage of each Tube for such emergencies. They are heat bombs. They fuse lead and rock."

Gripping the handle of his gun, Franks turned to Moss and Taylor.

"What do you say? We can't go back, but we can do a lot of damage, the fifteen of us. We have Bender guns. How about it?"

He looked around. The soldiers had wandered away again, back toward the exit of the building. They were standing outside, looking at the valley and the sky. A few of them were carefully climbing down the slope.

"Would you care to turn over your suits and guns?" the A-class leady asked politely. "The suits are uncomfortable and you'll have no need for weapons. The Russians have given up theirs, as you can see."

Fingers tensed on triggers. Four men in Russian uniforms were coming toward them from an aircraft that they suddenly realized had landed silently some distance away.

"Let them have it!" Franks shouted.

"They are unarmed," said the leady. "We brought them here so you could begin peace talks."

"We have no authority to speak for our country," Moss said stiffly.

"We do not mean diplomatic discussions," the leady explained. "There will be no more. The working out of daily problems of existence will teach you how to get along in the same world. It will not be easy, but it will be done."

* * * * *

The Russians halted and they faced each other with raw hostility.

"I am Colonel Borodoy and I regret giving up our guns," the senior Russian said. "You could have been the first Americans to be killed in almost eight years."

"Or the first Americans to kill," Franks corrected.

"No one would know of it except yourselves," the leady pointed out. "It would be useless heroism. Your real concern should be surviving on the surface. We have no food for you, you know."

Taylor put his gun in its holster. "They've done a neat job of neutralizing us, damn them. I propose we move into a city, start raising crops with the help of some leadys, and generally make ourselves comfortable." Drawing his lips tight over his teeth, he glared at the A-class leady. "Until our families can come up from undersurface, it's going to be pretty lonesome, but we'll have to manage."

"If I may make a suggestion," said another Russian uneasily. "We tried living in a city. It is too empty. It is also too hard to maintain for so few people. We finally settled in the most modern village we could find."

"Here in this country," a third Russian blurted. "We have much to learn from you."

The Americans abruptly found themselves laughing.

"You probably have a thing or two to teach us yourselves," said Taylor generously, "though I can't imagine what."

The Russian colonel grinned. "Would you join us in our village? It would make our work easier and give us company."

"Your village?" snapped Franks. "It's American, isn't it? It's ours!"

The leady stepped between them. "When our plans are completed, the term will be interchangeable. 'Ours' will eventually mean mankind's." It pointed at the aircraft, which was warming up. "The ship is waiting. Will you join each other in making a new home?"

The Russians waited while the Americans made up their minds.

"I see what the leadys mean about diplomacy becoming outmoded," Franks said at last. "People who work together don't need diplomats. They solve their problems on the operational level instead of at a conference table."

The leady led them toward the ship. "It is the goal of history, unifying the world. From family to tribe to city-state to nation to hemisphere, the direction has been toward unification. Now the hemispheres will be joined and —"

Taylor stopped listening and glanced back at the location of the Tube. Mary was undersurface there. He hated to leave her, even though he couldn't see her again until the Tube was unsealed. But then he shrugged and followed the others.

If this tiny amalgam of former enemies was a good example, it wouldn't be too long before he and Mary and the rest of humanity would be living on the surface like rational human beings instead of blindly hating moles.

"It has taken thousands of generations to achieve," the A-class leady concluded. "Hundreds of centuries of bloodshed and destruction. But each war was a step toward uniting mankind. And now the end is in sight: a world without war. But even that is only the beginning of a new stage of history."

"The conquest of space," breathed Colonel Borodoy.

"The meaning of life," Moss added.

"Eliminating hunger and poverty," said Taylor.

The leady opened the door of the ship. "All that and more. How much more? We cannot foresee it any more than the first men who formed a tribe could foresee this day. But it will be unimaginably great."

The door closed and the ship took off toward their new home.

The Unreconstructed M

1

The machine was a foot wide and two feet long; it looked like an oversized box of crackers. Silently, with great caution, it climbed the side of a concrete building; it had lowered two rubberized rollers and was now beginning the first phase of its job.

From its rear, a flake of blue enamel was exuded. The machine pressed the flake firmly against the rough concrete and then continued on. Its upward path carried it from vertical concrete to vertical steel: it had reached a window. The machine paused and produced a microscopic fragment of cloth fabric. The cloth, with great care, was embedded in the fitting of the steel window frame.

In the chill darkness, the machine was virtually invisible. The glow of a distant tangle of traffic briefly touched it, illuminated its polished hull, and departed. The machine resumed its work.

It projected a plastic pseudopodium and incinerated the pane of window glass. There was no response from within the gloomy apartment: nobody was home. The machine, now dulled with particles of glass-dust, crept over the steel frame and raised an inquisitive receptor.

While it received, it exerted precisely two hundred pounds pressure on the steel window frame; the frame obediently bent. Satisfied, the machine descended the inside of the wall to the moderately thick carpet. There it began the second phase of its job.

One single human hair -- follicle and speck of scalp included -- was deposited on the hardwood floor by the lamp. Not far from the piano, two dried grains of tobacco were ceremoniously laid out. The machine waited an interval of ten seconds and then, as an internal section of magnetic tape clicked into place, it suddenly said, "Ugh! Damn it. . ."

Curiously, its voice was husky and masculine.

The machine made its way to the closet door, which was locked. Climbing the wood surface, the machine reached the lock mechanism, and, inserting a thin section of itself, caressed the tumblers back. Behind the row of coats was a small mound of batteries and wires: a self-powered video recorder. The machine destroyed the reservoir of film -- which was vital -- and then, as it left the closet, expelled a drop of blood on the jagged tangle that had been the lens-scanner. The drop of blood was even more vital.

While the machine was pressing the artificial outline of a heel mark into the greasy film that covered the flooring of the closet, a sharp sound came from the hallway. The machine ceased its work and became rigid. A moment later a small, middle-aged man entered the apartment, coat over one arm, briefcase in the other.

"Good God," he said, stopping instantly as he saw the machine. "What are you?"

The machine lifted the nozzle of its front section and shot an explosive pellet at the man's half-bald head. The pellet traveled into the skull and detonated. Still clutching his coat and briefcase, bewildered expression on his face, the man collapsed to the rug. His glasses, broken, lay twisted beside his ear. His body stirred a little, twitched, and then was satisfactorily quiet.

Only two steps remained to the job, now that the main part was done. The machine deposited a bit of burnt match in one of the spotless ashtrays resting on the mantel, and entered the kitchen to search for a water glass. It was starting up the side of the sink when the noise of human voices startled it.

"This is the apartment," a voice said, clear and close.

"Get ready -- he ought to still be here." Another voice, a man's voice, like the first. The hall door was pushed open and two individuals in heavy overcoats sprinted purposefully into the apartment. At their approach, the machine dropped to the kitchen floor, the water glass forgotten. Something had gone wrong. Its rectangular outline flowed and wavered; pulling itself into an upright package it fused its shape into that of a conventional TV unit.

It was holding that emergency form when one of the men -- tall, red-haired -- peered briefly into the kitchen.

"Nobody in here," the man declared, and hurried on.

"The window," his companion said, panting. Two more figures entered the apartment, an entire crew. "The glass is gone -- missing. He got in that way."

"But he's gone." The red-haired man reappeared at the kitchen door; he snapped on the light and entered, a gun visible in his hand. "Strange ...we got here right away, as soon as we picked up the rattle." Suspiciously, he examined his wristwatch. "Rosenburg's been dead only a few seconds . . . how could he have got out again so fast?"

Standing in the street entrance, Edward Ackers listened to the voice. During the last half hour the voice had taken on a carping, nagging whine; sinking almost to inaudibility, it plodded along, mechanically turning out its message of complaint.

"You're tired," Ackers said. "Go home. Take a hot bath."

"No," the voice said, interrupting its tirade. The locus of the voice was a large illuminated blob on the dark sidewalk, a few yards to Acker's right. The revolving neon sign read:

BANISH IT!

Thirty times -- he had counted -- within the last few minutes the sign had captured a passerby and the man in the booth had begun his harangue. Beyond the booth were several theaters and restaurants: the booth was well-situated.

But it wasn't for the crowd that the booth had been erected. It was for Ackers and the offices behind him; the tirade was aimed directly at the Interior Department. The nagging racket had gone on so many months that Ackers was scarcely aware of it. Rain on the roof. Traffic noises. He yawned, folded his arms, and waited.

"Banish it," the voice complained peevishly. "Come on, Ackers. Say something; do something."

"I'm waiting," Ackers said complacently.

A group of middle-class citizens passed the booth and were handed leaflets. The citizens scattered the leaflets after them, and Ackers laughed.

"Don't laugh," the voice muttered. "It's not funny; it costs us money to print those."

"Your personal money?" Ackers inquired.

"Partly." Garth was lonely, tonight. "What are you waiting for? What's happened? I saw a police team leave your roof a few minutes ago . . . ?

"We may take in somebody," Ackers said, "there's been a killing."

Down the dark sidewalk the man stirred in his dreary propaganda booth. "Oh?" Harvey Garth's voice came. He leaned forward and the two looked directly at each other: Ackers, carefully-groomed, well-fed, wearing a respectable overcoat. . . Garth, a thin man, much younger, with a lean, hungry face composed mostly of nose and forehead.

"So you see," Ackers told him, "we do need the system. Don't be Utopian."

"A man is murdered; and you rectify the moral imbalance by killing the killer." Garth's protesting voice rose in a bleak spasm. "Banish it! Banish the system that condemns men to certain extinction!"

"Get your leaflets here," Ackers parodied dryly. "And your slogans. Either or both. What would you suggest in place of the system?"

Garth's voice was proud with conviction. "Education."

Amused, Ackers asked: "Is that all? You think that would stop anti-social activity? Criminals just don't -- *know* better?"

"And psychotherapy, of course." His projected face bony and intense, Garth peered out of his booth like an aroused turtle. "They're sick . . . that's why they commit crimes, healthy men don't commit crimes. And you compound it; you create a sick society of punitive cruelty." He waggled an accusing finger. "You're the real culprit, you and the whole Interior Department. You and the whole Banishment System."

Again and again the neon sign blinked BANISH it! Meaning, of course, the system of compulsory ostracism for felons, the machinery that projected a condemned human being into some random backwater region of the sidereal universe, into some remote and out-of-the-way corner where he would be of no harm.

"No harm to us, anyhow," Ackers mused aloud.

Garth spoke the familiar argument. "Yes, but what about the local inhabitants?"

Too bad about the local inhabitants. Anyhow, the banished victim spent his energy and time trying to find a way back to the Sol System. If he got back before old age caught up with him he was readmitted by society. Quite a challenge . . . especially to some cosmopolite who had never set foot outside Greater New York. There were -- probably -- many involuntary expatriates cutting grain in odd fields with primitive sickles. The remote sections of the universe seemed composed mostly of dank rural cultures, isolated agrarian enclaves typified by small-time bartering of fruit and vegetables and handmade artifacts.

"Did you know," Ackers said, "that in the Age of Monarchs, a pickpocket was usually hanged?"

"Banish it," Garth continued monotonously, sinking back into his booth. The sign revolved; leaflets were passed out. And Ackers impatiently watched the late-evening street for sign of the hospital truck.

He knew Heimie Rosenburg. A sweeter little guy there never was. . . although Heimie had been mixed up in one of the sprawling slave combines that illegally transported settlers to outsystem fertile planets. Between them, the two largest slavers had settled virtually the entire Sirius System. Four out of six emigrants were hustled out in carriers registered as "freighters." It was hard to picture gentle little Heimie Rosenburg as a business agent for Tirol Enterprises, but there it was.

As he waited, Ackers conjectured on Heimie's murder. Probably one element of the incessant subterranean war going on between Paul Tirol and his major rival, David Lantano, was a brilliant and energetic newcomer . . . but murder was anybody's game. It all depended on how it was done; it could be commercial hack or the purest art.

"Here comes something," Garth's voice sounded, carried to his inner ear by the delicate output transformers of the booth's equipment. "Looks like a freezer."

It was; the hospital truck had arrived. Ackers stepped forward as the truck halted and the back was let down.

"How soon did you get there?" he asked the cop who jumped heavily to the pavement.

"Right away," the cop answered, "but no sign of the killer. I don't think we're going to get Heimie back . . . they got him dead-center, right in the cerebellum. Expert work, no amateur stuff."

Disappointed, Ackers clambered into the hospital truck to inspect for himself.

Very tiny and still, Heimie Rosenburg lay on his back, arms at his sides, gazing sightlessly up at the roof of the truck. On his face remained the expression of bewildered wonder. Somebody -- one of the cops -- had placed his bent glasses in his clenched hand. In falling he had cut his cheek. The destroyed portion of his skull was covered by a moist plastic web.

"Who's back at the apartment?" Ackers asked presently.

"The rest of my crew," the cop answered. "And an independent researcher. Leroy Beam."

"Him," Ackers said, with aversion. "How is it he showed up?"

"Caught the rattle, too, happened to be passing with his rig. Poor Heimie had an awful big booster on that rattle . . . I'm surprised it wasn't picked up here at the main offices."

"They say Heimie had a high anxiety level," Ackers said. "Bugs all over his apartment. You're starting to collect evidence?"

"The teams are moving in," the cop said. "We should begin getting specifications in half an hour. The killer knocked out the vid bug set up in the closet. But --" He grinned. "He cut himself breaking the circuit. A drop of blood, right on the wiring; it looks promising."

At the apartment, Leroy Beam watched the Interior police begin their analysis. They worked smoothly and thoroughly, but Beam was dissatisfied.

His original impression remained: he was suspicious. Nobody could have gotten away so quickly. Heimie had died, and his death -- the cessation of his neural pattern -- had triggered off an automatic squawk. A rattle didn't particularly protect its owner, but its existence ensured (or usually ensured) detection of the murderer. Why had it failed Heimie?

Prowling moodily, Leroy Beam entered the kitchen for the second time. There, on the floor by the sink, was a small portable TV unit, the kind popular with the sporting set: a gaudy little packet of plastic and knobs and multi-tinted lenses.

"Why this?" Beam asked, as one of the cops plodded past him. "This TV unit sitting here on the kitchen floor. It's out of place."

The cop ignored him. In the living room, elaborate police detection equipment was scraping the various surfaces inch by inch. In the half hour since Heimie's death, a number of specifications had been logged. First, the drop of blood on the damaged vid wiring. Second, a hazy heel mark where the murderer had stepped. Third, a bit of burnt match in the ashtray. More were expected; the analysis had only begun.

It usually took nine specifications to delineate the single individual. Leroy Beam glanced cautiously around him. None of the cops was watching, so he bent down and picked up the TV unit; it felt ordinary. He clicked the *on* switch and waited. Nothing happened; no image formed. Strange.

He was holding it upside down, trying to see the inner chassis, when Edward Ackers from Interior entered the apartment. Quickly, Beam stuffed the TV unit into the pocket of his heavy overcoat.

"What are you doing here?" Ackers said.

"Seeking," Beam answered, wondering if Ackers noticed his tubby bulge. "I'm in business, too."

"Did you know Heimie?"

"By reputation," Beam answered vaguely. "Tied in with Tirol's combine, I hear; some sort of front man. Had an office on Fifth Avenue."

"Swank place, like the rest of those Fifth Avenue feather merchants." Ackers went on into the living room to watch detectors gather up evidence.

There was a vast nearsightedness to the wedge grinding ponderously across the carpet. It was scrutinizing at a microscopic level, and its field was sharply curtailed. As fast as material was obtained, it was relayed to the Interior offices, to the aggregate file banks where the civil population was represented by a series of punch cards, cross-indexed infinitely.

Lifting the telephone, Ackers called his wife. "I won't be home," he told her. "Business."

A lag and then Ellen responded. "Oh?" she said distantly. "Well, thanks for letting me know."

Over in the corner, two members of the police crew were delightedly examining a new discovery, valid enough to be a specification. "I'll call you again," he said hurriedly to Ellen, "before I leave. Goodbye."

"Goodbye," Ellen said curtly, and managed to hang up before he did. The new discovery was the undamaged aud bug, which was mounted under the floor lamp. A continuous magnetic tape -- still in motion -- gleamed amiably; the murder episode had been recorded sound-wise in its entirety.

"Everything," a cop said gleefully to Ackers. "It was going before Heimie got home."

"You played it back?"

"A portion. There's a couple words spoken by the murderer, should be enough."

Ackers got in touch with Interior. "Have the specifications on the Rosenburg case been fed, yet?"

"Just the first," the attendant answered. "The file discriminates the usual massive category -- about six billion names."

Ten minutes later the second specification was fed to the files. Persons with type O blood, with size 11 1/2 shoes, numbered slightly over a billion. The third specification brought in the element of smoker-nonsmoker. That dropped the number to less than a billion, but not much less. Most adults smoked.

"The aud tape will drop it fast," Leroy Beam commented, standing beside Ackers, his arms folded to conceal his bulging coat. "Ought to be able to get age, at least."

The aud tape, analyzed, gave thirty to forty years as the conjectured age. And -- timbre analysis -- a man of perhaps two hundred pounds. A little later the bent steel window frame was examined, and the warp noted. It jibed with the specification of the aud tape. There were now six specifications, including that of sex (male). The number of persons in the in-group was falling rapidly.

"It won't be long," Ackers said genially. "And if he tacked one of those little buckets to the building side, we'll have a paint scrape."

Beam said: "I'm leaving. Good luck."

"Stick around."

"Sorry." Beam moved toward the hall door. "This is yours, not mine. I've got my own business to attend to. . . I'm doing research for a hot-shot nonferrous mining concern."

Ackers eyed his coat. "Are you pregnant?"

"Not that I know of," Beam said, coloring. "I've led a good clean life." Awkwardly, he patted his coat. "You mean this?"

By the window, one of the police gave a triumphant yap. The two bits of pipe tobacco had been discovered: a refinement for the third specification. "Excellent," Ackers said, turning away from Beam and momentarily forgetting him.

Beam left.

Very shortly he was driving across town toward his own labs, the small and independent research outfit that he headed, unsupported by a government grant. Resting on the seat beside him was the portable TV unit; it was still silent.

"First of all," Beam's gowned technician declared, "it has a power supply approximately seventy times that of a portable TV pack. We picked up the Gamma radiation." He displayed the usual detector. "So you're right, it's not a TV set"

Gingerly, Beam lifted the small unit from the lab bench. Five hours had passed, and still he knew nothing about it. Taking firm hold of the back he pulled with all his strength. The back refused to come off. It wasn't stuck: there were no seams. The back was not a back; it only looked like a back.

"Then what is it?" he asked.

"Could be lots of things," the technician said noncommittally; he had been roused from the privacy of his home, and it was now two-thirty in the morning. "Could be some sort of scanning equipment. A bomb. A weapon. Any kind of gadget." Laboriously, Beam felt the unit all over, searching for a flaw in the surface. "It's uniform," he murmured. "A single surface."

"You bet. The breaks are false -- it's a poured substance. And," the technician added, "it's hard. I tried to chip off a representative sample but --" He gestured. "No results."

"Guaranteed not to shatter when dropped," Beam said absently. "New extra-tough plastic." He shook the unit energetically; the muted noise of metal parts in motion reached his ear. "It's full of guts."

"We'll get it open," the technician promised, "but not tonight."

Beam replaced the unit on the bench. He could, with bad luck, work days on this one item -- to discover, after all, that it had nothing to do with the murder of Heimie Rosenburg. On the other hand . . .

"Drill me a hole in it," he instructed. "So we can see it."

His technician protested: "I drilled; the drill broke. I've sent out for an improved density. This substance is imported; somebody hooked it from a white dwarf system. It was conceived under stupendous pressure."

"You're stalling," Beam said, irritated. "That's how they talk in the advertising media."

The technician shrugged. "Anyhow, it's extra hard. A naturally-evolved element, or an artificially-processed product from somebody's labs. Who has funds to develop a metal like this?"

"One of the big slavers," Beam said. "That's where the wealth winds up. And they hop around to various systems . . . they'd have access to raw materials. Special ores."

"Can't I go home?" the technician asked. "What's so important about this?"

"This device either killed or helped kill Heimie Rosenburg. We'll sit here, you and I, until we get it open." Beam seated himself and began examining the check sheet showing which tests had been applied. "Sooner or later it'll fly open like a clam -- if you can remember that far back."

Behind them, a warning bell sounded.

"Somebody in the anteroom," Beam said, surprised and wary. "At two-thirty?" He got up and made his way down the dark hall to the front of the building. Probably it was Ackers. His conscience stirred guiltily: somebody had logged the absence of the TV unit.

But it was not Ackers.

Waiting humbly in the cold, deserted anteroom was Paul Tirol; with him was an attractive young woman unknown to Beam. Tirol's wrinkled face broke into smiles, and he extended a hearty hand. "Beam," he said. They shook. "Your front door said you were down here. Still working?"

Guardedly, wondering who the woman was and what Tirol wanted, Beam said: "Catching up on some slipshod errors. Whole firm's going broke."

Tirol laughed indulgently. "Always a japer." His deep-set eyes darted; Tirol was a powerfully-built person, older than most, with a somber, intensely-creased face. "Have room for a few contracts? I thought I might slip a few jobs your way. . . if you're open."

"I'm always open," Beam countered, blocking Tirol's view of the lab proper. The door, anyhow, had slid itself shut. Tirol had been Heimie's boss . . . he no doubt felt entitled to all extant information on the murder. Who did it? When? How? Why? But that didn't explain why he was *here*.

"Terrible thing," Tirol said crudely. He made no move to introduce the woman; she had retired to the couch to light a cigarette. She was slender, with mahogany-colored hair; she wore a blue coat, and a kerchief tied around her head.

"Yes," Beam agreed. "Terrible."

"You were there, I understand."

That explained some of it. "Well," Beam conceded, "I showed up."

"But you didn't actually see it?"

"No," Beam admitted, "nobody saw it. Interior is collecting specification material. They should have it down to one card before morning."

Visibly, Tirol relaxed. "I'm glad of that. I'd hate to see the vicious criminal escape. Banishment's too good for him. He ought to be gassed."

"Barbarism," Beam murmured dryly. "The days of the gas chamber. Medieval."

Tirol peered past him. "You're working on --" Now he was overtly beginning to pry. "Come now, Leroy. Heimie Rosenburg -- God bless his soul -- was killed tonight and tonight I find you burning the midnight oil. You can talk openly with me; you've got something relevant to his death, haven't you?"

"That's Ackers you're thinking of."

Tirol chuckled. "Can I take a look?"

"Not until you start paying me; I'm not on your books yet."

In a strained, unnatural voice, Tirol bleated: "I want it."

Puzzled, Beam said: "You want what?"

With a grotesque shudder, Tirol blundered forward, shoved Beam aside, and groped for the door. The door flew open and Tirol started noisily down the dark corridor, feeling his way by instinct toward the research labs.

"Hey!" Beam shouted, outraged. He sprinted after the older man, reached the inner door, and prepared to fight it out. He was shaking, partly with amazement, partly with anger. "What the hell?" he demanded breathlessly. "You don't own me!"

Behind him the door mysteriously gave way. Foolishly, he sprawled backward, half-falling into the lab. There, stricken with helpless paralysis, was his technician. And, coming across the floor of the lab was something small and metallic. It looked like an oversized box of crackers, and it was going lickety-split toward Tirol. The object -- metal and gleaming -- hopped up into Tirol's arms, and the old man turned and lumbered back up the hall to the anteroom.

"What was it?" the technician said, coming to life.

Ignoring him, Beam hurried after Tirol. "He's got it!" he yelled futilely.

"It --" the technician mumbled. "It was the TV set. And it *ran.*"

2

The file banks at Interior were in agitated flux.

The process of creating a more and more restricted category was tedious, and it took time. Most of the Interior staff had gone home to bed; it was almost three in the morning, and the corridors and offices were deserted. A few mechanical cleaning devices crept here and there in the darkness. The sole source of life was the study chamber of the file banks. Edward Ackers sat patiently waiting for the results, waiting for specifications to come in, and for the file machinery to process them.

To his right a few Interior police played a benign lottery and waited stoically to be sent out for the pick-up. The lines of communication to Heimie Rosenburg's apartment buzzed ceaselessly. Down the street, along the bleak sidewalk, Harvey Garth was still at his propaganda booth, still flashing his BANISH it! sign and muttering in people's ears. There were virtually no passersby, now, but Garth went on. He was tireless; he never gave up.

"Psychopath," Ackers said resentfully. Even where he sat, six floors up, the tinny, carping voice reached his middle ear.

"Take him in," one of the game-playing cops suggested. The game, intricate and devious, was a version of a Centaurian III practice. "We can revoke his vendor's license."

Ackers had, when there was nothing else to do, concocted and refined an indictment of Garth, a sort of lay analysis of the man's mental aberrations. He enjoyed playing the psychoanalytic game; it gave him a sense of power.

Garth, Harvey

Prominent compulsive syndrome. Has assumed role of ideological anarchist, opposing legal and social system. No rational expression, only repetition of key words and phrases. Idee fixe is *Banish the banishment system.* Cause dominates life. Rigid fanatic, probably of manic type, since. . .

Ackers let the sentence go, since he didn't really know what the structure of the manic type was. Anyhow, the analysis was excellent, and someday it would be resting in an official slot instead of merely drifting through his mind. And, when that happened, the annoying voice would conclude.

"Big turmoil," Garth droned. "Banishment system in vast upheaval. . . crisis moment has arrived."

"Why crisis?" Ackers asked aloud.

Down below on the pavement Garth responded. "All your machines are humming. Grand excitement reigns. Somebody's head will be in the basket before sun-up." His voice trailed off in a weary blur. "Intrigue and murder. Corpses . . . the police scurry and a beautiful woman lurks." To his analysis Ackers added an amplifying clause.

. . .Garth's talents are warped by his compulsive sense of *mission.* Having designed an ingenious communication device he sees only its propaganda possibility. Whereas Garth's voice-ear mechanism could be put to work for All Humanity.

That pleased him. Ackers got up and wandered over to the attendant operating the file. "How's it coming?" he asked.

"Here's the situation," the attendant said. There was a line of gray stubble smeared over his chin, and he was bleary-eyed. "We're gradually paring it down."

Ackers, as he resumed his seat, wished he were back in the days of the almighty fingerprint. But a print hadn't shown up in months; a thousand techniques existed for print-removal and print alteration. There was no single specification capable, in itself, of delineating the individual. A composite was needed, a gestalt of the assembled data.

1) blood sample (type O) 6,139,481,601
2) shoe size (11 1/2) 1,268,303,431
3) smoker 791,992,386
3a) smoker (pipe) 52,774,853

4) sex (male) 26,449,094
5) age (30-40 years) 9,221,397
6) weight (200 lbs) 488,290
7) fabric of clothing 17,459
8) hair variety 866
9) ownership of utilized weapon 40

A vivid picture was emerging from the data. Ackers could see him clearly. The man was practically standing there, in front of his desk. A fairly young man, somewhat heavy, a man who smoked a pipe and wore an extremely expensive tweed suit. An individual created by nine specifications; no tenth had been listed because no more data of specification level had been found.

Now, according to the report, the apartment had been thoroughly searched. The detection equipment was going outdoors.

"One more should do it," Ackers said, returning the report to the attendant. He wondered if it would come in and how long it would take.

To waste time he telephoned his wife, but instead of getting Ellen he got the automatic response circuit. "Yes, sir," it told him. "Mrs. Ackers has retired for the night. You may state a thirty-second message which will be transcribed for her attention tomorrow morning. Thank you."

Ackers raged at the mechanism futilely and then hung up. He wondered if Ellen were really in bed; maybe she had, as often before, slipped out. But, after all, it was almost three o'clock in the morning. Any sane person would be asleep: only he and Garth were still at their little stations, performing their vital duties.

What had Garth meant by a *"beautiful woman"*?

"Mr. Ackers," the attendant said, "there's a tenth specification coming in over the wires."

Hopefully, Ackers gazed up at the file bank. He could see nothing, of course; the actual mechanism occupied the underground levels of the building, and all that existed here was the input receptors and throw-out slots. But just looking at the machinery was in itself comforting. At this moment the bank was accepting the tenth piece of material. In a moment he would know how many citizens fell into the ten categories . . . he would know if already he had a group small enough to be sorted one by one.

"Here it is," the attendant said, pushing the report to him.

Type of utilized vehicle (color) 7

"My God," Ackers said mildly. "That's low enough. Seven persons -- we can go to work."

"You want the seven cards popped?"

"Pop them," Ackers said.

A moment later, the throw-out slot deposited seven neat white cards in the tray. The attendant passed them to Ackers and he quickly riffled them. The next step was personal motive and proximity: items that had to be gotten from the suspects themselves.

Of the seven names six meant nothing to him. Two lived on Venus, one in the Centaurus System, one was somewhere in Sirius, one was in the hospital, and one lived in the Soviet Union. The seventh, however, lived within a few miles, on the outskirts of New York.

LANTANO, DAVID

That clinched it. The gestalt, in Ackers' mind, locked clearly in place; the image hardened to reality. He had half expected, even prayed to see Lantano's card brought up.

"Here's your pick-up," he said shakily to the game-playing cops. "Better get as large a team together as possible, this one won't be easy." Momentously, he added: "Maybe I'd better come along."

Beam reached the anteroom of his lab as the ancient figure of Paul Tirol disappeared out the street door and onto the dark sidewalk. The young woman, trotting ahead of him, had climbed into a parked car and started it forward; as Tirol emerged, she swept him up and at once departed.

Panting, Beam stood impotently collecting himself on the deserted pavement. The ersatz TV unit was gone; now he had nothing. Aimlessly, he began to run down the street. His heels echoed loudly in the cold silence. No sign of them; no sign of anything.

"I'll be damned," he said, with almost religious awe. The unit -- a robot device of obvious complexity -- clearly belonged to Paul Tirol; as soon as it had identified his presence it had sprinted gladly to him. For. . . protection?

It had killed Heimie; and it belonged to Tirol. So, by a novel and indirect method, Tirol had murdered his employee, his Fifth Avenue front man. At a rough guess, such a highly-organized robot would cost in the neighborhood of a hundred thousand dollars.

A lot of money, considering that murder was the easiest of criminal acts. Why not hire an itinerant goon with a crowbar?

Beam started slowly back toward his lab. Then, abruptly, he changed his mind and turned in the direction of the business area. When a free-wheeling cab came by, he hailed it and clambered in.

"Where to, sport?" the starter at cab relay asked. City cabs were guided by remote control from one central source.

He gave the name of a specific bar. Settling back against the seat he pondered. Anybody could commit a murder; an expensive, complicated machine wasn't necessary.

The machine had been built to do something else. The murder of Heimie Rosenburg was incidental.

Against the nocturnal skyline, a huge stone residence loomed. Ackers inspected it from a distance. There were no lights burning; everything was locked up tight. Spread out before the house was an acre of grass. David Lantano was probably the last person on Earth to own an acre of grass outright; it was less expensive to buy an entire planet in some other system.

"Let's go," Ackers commanded; disgusted by such opulence, he deliberately trampled through a bed of roses on his way up the wide porch steps. Behind him flowed the team of shock-police.

"Gosh," Lantano rumbled, when he had been roused from his bed. He was a kindly-looking, rather youthful fat man, wearing now an abundant silk dressing robe. He would have seemed more in place as director of a boys' summer camp; there was an expression of perpetual good humor on his soft, sagging face. "What's wrong, officer?"

Ackers loathed being called officer. "You're under arrest," he stated.

"Me?" Lantano echoed feebly. "Hey, officer, I've got lawyers to take care of these things." He yawned voluminously. "Care for some coffee?" Stupidly, he began puttering around his front room, fixing a pot.

It had been years since Ackers had splurged and bought himself a cup of coffee. With Terran land covered by dense industrial and residential installations there was no room for crops, and coffee had refused to "take" in any other system. Lantano probably grew his somewhere on an illicit plantation in South America -- the pickers probably believed they had been transported to some remote colony.

"No thanks," Ackers said. "Let's get going."

Still dazed, Lantano plopped himself down in an easy chair and regarded Ackers with alarm. "You're serious." Gradually his expression faded; he seemed to be drifting back to sleep. "Who?" he murmured distantly.

"Heimie Rosenburg."

"No kidding." Lantano shook his head listlessly. "I always wanted him in my company. Heimie's got real charm. Had, I mean."

It made Ackers nervous to remain here in the vast lush mansion. The coffee was heating, and the smell of it tickled his nose. And, heaven forbid -- there on the table was a basket *of apricots*.

"Peaches," Lantano corrected, noticing his fixed stare. "Help yourself."

"Where -- did you get them?"

Lantano shrugged. "Synthetic dome. Hydroponics. I forget where . . . I don't have a technical mind."

"You know what the fine is for possessing natural fruit?"

"Look," Lantano said earnestly, clasping his mushy hands together. "Give me the details on this affair, and I'll prove to you I had nothing to do with it. Come on, officer."

"Ackers," Ackers said.

"Okay, Ackers. I thought I recognized you, but I wasn't sure; didn't want to make a fool of myself. When was Heimie killed?"

Grudgingly, Ackers gave him the pertinent information.

For a time Lantano was silent. Then, slowly, gravely, he said: "You better look at those seven cards again. One of those fellows isn't in the Sirius System . . . he's back here."

Ackers calculated the chances of successfully banishing a man of David Lantano's importance. His organization -- Interplay Export -- had fingers all over the galaxy; there'd be search crews going out like bees. But nobody went out banishment distance. The condemned, temporarily ionized, rendered in terms of charged particles of energy, radiated outward at the velocity of light. This was an experimental technique that had failed; it worked only one way.

"Consider," Lantano said thoughtfully. "If I *was* going to kill Heimie -- *would I do it myself?* You're not being logical, Ackers. I'd send somebody." He pointed a fleshy finger at Ackers. "You imagine I'd risk my own life? I know you pick up everybody . . . you usually turn up enough specifications."

"We have ten on you," Ackers said briskly.

"So you're going to banish me?"

"If you're guilty, you'll have to face banishment like anyone else. Your particular prestige has no bearing."

Nettled, Ackers added, "Obviously, you'll be released. You'll have plenty of opportunity to prove your innocence; you can question each of the ten specifications in turn."

He started to go on and describe the general process of court procedure employed in the twenty-first century, but something made him pause. David Lantano and his chair seemed to be gradually sinking into the floor. Was it an illusion? Blinking, Ackers rubbed his eyes and peered. At the same time, one of the policemen yelped a warning of dismay; Lantano was quietly leaving them.

"Come back!" Ackers demanded; he leaped forward and grabbed hold of the chair. Hurriedly, one of his men shorted out the power supply of the building; the chair ceased descending and groaned to a halt. Only Lantano's head was visible above the floor level. He was almost entirely submerged in a concealed escape shaft.

"What seedy, useless -- " Ackers began.

"I know," Lantano admitted, making no move to drag himself up. He seemed resigned; his mind was again off in clouds of contemplation. "I hope we can clear all this up. Evidently I'm being framed. Tirol got somebody who looks like me, somebody to go in and murder Heimie."

Ackers and the police crew helped him up from his depressed chair. He gave no resistance; he was too deep in his brooding.

The cab let Leroy Beam off in front of the bar. To his right, in the next block, was the Interior Building. . . and, on the sidewalk, the opaque blob that was Harvey Garth's propaganda booth.

Entering the bar, Beam found a table in the back and seated himself. Already he could pick up the faint, distorted murmur of Garth's reflections. Garth, speaking to himself in a directionless blur, was not yet aware of him.

"Banish it," Garth was saying. "Banish all of them. Bunch of crooks and thieves." Garth, in the miasma of his booth, was rambling vitriolically.

"What's going on?" Beam asked. "What's the latest?"

Garth's monologue broke off as he focussed his attention on Beam. "You in there? In the bar?"

"I want to find out about Heimie's death."

"Yes," Garth said. "He's dead; the files are moving, kicking out cards."

"When I left Heimie's apartment," Beam said, "they had turned up six specifications." He punched a button on the drink selector and dropped in a token.

"That must have been earlier," Garth said; "they've got more."

"How many?"

"Ten in all."

Ten. That was usually enough. And all ten of them laid out by a robot device . . . a little procession of hints strewn along its path: between the concrete side of the building and the dead body of Heimie Rosenburg.

"That's lucky," he said speculatively. "Helps out Ackers."

"Since you're paying me," Garth said, "I'll tell you the rest. They've already gone out on their pick-up: Ackers went along."

Then the device had been successful. Up to a point, at least. He was sure of one thing: the device should have been out of the apartment. Tirol hadn't known about Heimie's death rattle; Heimie had been wise enough to do the installation privately.

Had the rattle not brought persons into the apartment, the device would have scuttled out and returned to Tirol. Then, no doubt, Tirol would have detonated it. Nothing would remain to indicate that a machine could lay down a trail of synthetic clues: blood type, fabric, pipe tobacco, hair... all the rest, and all spurious.

"Who's the pick-up on?" Beam asked.

"David Lantano."

Beam winced. "Naturally. That's what the whole thing's about; he's being framed!"

Garth was indifferent; he was a hired employee, stationed by the pool of independent researchers to siphon information from the Interior Department. He had no actual interest in politics; his *Banish It!* was sheer window-dressing.

"I know it's a frame," Beam said, "and so does Lantano. But neither of us can prove it. . . unless Lantano has an absolutely airtight alibi."

"Banish it," Garth murmured, reverting to his routine. A small group of late-retiring citizens had strolled past his booth, and he was masking his conversation with Beam. The conversation, directed to the one listener, was inaudible to everyone else; but it was better not to take risks. Sometimes, very close to the booth, there was an audible feedback of the signal.

Hunched over his drink, Leroy Beam contemplated the various items he could try. He could inform Lantano's organization, which existed relatively intact. . . but the result would be epic civil war. And, in addition, he didn't really care if Lantano was framed; it was all the same to him. Sooner or later one of the big slavers had to absorb the other: cartel is the natural conclusion of big business. With Lantano gone, Tirol would painlessly swallow his organization; everybody would be working at his desk as always.

On the other hand, there might someday be a device -- now half-completed in Tirol's basement -- that left a trail of *Leroy Beam* clues. Once the idea caught on, there was no particular end.

"And I had the damn thing," he said fruitlessly. "I hammered on it for five hours. It was a TV unit, then, but it was still the device that killed Heimie."

"You're positive it's gone?"

"It's not only gone -- it's out of existence. Unless she wrecked the car driving Tirol home."

"She?" Garth asked.

"The woman." Beam pondered. "She saw it. Or she knew about it; she was with him." But, unfortunately, he had no idea who the woman might be.

"What'd she look like?" Garth asked.

"Tall, mahogany hair. Very nervous mouth."

"I didn't realize she was working with him openly. They must have really needed the device." Garth added: "You didn't identify her? I guess there's no reason why you should; she's kept out of sight."

"Who is she?"

"That's Ellen Ackers."

Beam laughed sharply. "And she's driving Paul Tirol around?"

"She's -- well, she's driving Tirol around, yes. You can put it that way."

"How long?"

"I thought you were in on it. She and Ackers split up; that was last year. But he wouldn't let her leave; he wouldn't give her a divorce. Afraid of the publicity. Very important to keep up respectability. . . keep the shirt fully stuffed."

"He knows about Paul Tirol and her?"

"Of course not. He knows she's -- spiritually hooked up. But he doesn't care . . . as long as she keeps it quiet. It's his position he's thinking about."

"If Ackers found out," Beam murmured. "If he saw the link between his wife and Tirol. . . he'd ignore his ten interoffice memos. He'd *want* to haul in Tirol. The hell with the evidence; he could always collect that later." Beam pushed away his drink; the glass was empty anyhow. "Where is Ackers?"

"I told you. Out at Lantano's place, picking him up."

"He'd come back here? He wouldn't go home?"

"Naturally he'd come back here." Garth was silent a moment. "I see a couple of Interior vans turning into the garage ramp. That's probably the pick-up crew returning."

Beam waited tensely. "Is Ackers along?"

"Yes, he's there. *Banish It!*" Garth's voice rose in stentorian frenzy. "*Banish the system of Banishment! Root out the crooks and pirates!*"

Sliding to his feet, Beam left the bar.

A dull light showed in the rear of Edward Ackers' apartment: probably the kitchen light. The front door was locked. Standing in the carpeted hallway, Beam skillfully tilted with the door mechanism. It was geared to respond to specific neural patterns: those of its owners and a limited circle of friends. For him there was no activity.

Kneeling down, Beam switched on a pocket oscillator and started sine wave emission. Gradually, he increased the frequency. At perhaps 150,000 cps the lock guiltily clicked; that was all he needed. Switching the oscillator off, he rummaged through his supply of skeleton patterns until he located the closet cylinder. Slipped into the turret of the oscillator, the cylinder emitted a synthetic neural pattern close enough to the real thing to affect the lock.

The door swung open. Beam entered.

In half-darkness the living room seemed modest and tasteful. Ellen Ackers was an adequate housekeeper. Beam listened. Was she home at all? And if so, where? Awake? Asleep?

He peeped into the bedroom. There was the bed, but nobody was in it.

If she wasn't here she was at Tirol's. But he didn't intend to follow her; this was as far as he cared to risk.

He inspected the dining room. Empty. The kitchen was empty, too. Next came an upholstered general-purpose rumpus room; on one side was a gaudy bar and on the other a wall-to-wall couch. Tossed on the couch was a woman's coat, purse, gloves. Familiar clothes: Ellen Ackers had worn them. So she had come here after leaving his research lab.

The only room left was the bathroom. He fumbled with the knob; it was locked from the inside. There was no sound, but somebody was on the other side of the door. He could sense her in there.

"Ellen," he said, against the panelling. "Mrs. Ellen Ackers; is that you?"

No answer. He could sense her not making any sound at all: a stifled, frantic silence.

While he was kneeling down, fooling with his pocketful of magnetic lock-pullers, an explosive pellet burst through the door at head level and splattered into the plaster of the wall beyond.

Instantly the door flew open; there stood Ellen Ackers, her face distorted with fright. One of her husband's government pistols was clenched in her small, bony hand. She was less than a foot from him. Without getting up, Beam grabbed her wrist; she fired over his head, and then the two of them deteriorated into harsh, labored breathing.

"Come on," Beam managed finally. The nozzle of the gun was literally brushing the top of his head. To kill him, she would have to pull the pistol back against her. But he didn't let her; he kept hold of her wrist until finally, reluctantly, she dropped the gun. It clattered to the floor and he got stiffly up.

"You were sitting down," she whispered, in a stricken, accusing voice.

"Kneeling down: picking the lock. I'm glad you aimed for my brain." He picked up the gun and succeeded in getting it into his overcoat pocket; his hands were shaking.

Ellen Ackers gazed at him starkly; her eyes were huge and dark, and her face was an ugly white. Her skin had a dead cast, as if it were artificial, totally dry, thoroughly sifted with talc. She seemed on the verge of hysteria; a harsh, muffled shudder struggled up inside her, lodging finally in her throat. She tried to speak but only a rasping noise came out.

"Gee, lady," Beam said, embarrassed. "Come in the kitchen and sit down."

She stared at him as if he had said something incredible or obscene or miraculous; he wasn't sure which.

"Come on." He tried to take hold of her arm but she jerked frantically away. She had on a simple green suit, and in it she looked very nice; a little too thin and terribly tense, but still attractive. She had on expensive earrings, an imported stone that seemed always in motion . . . but otherwise her outfit was austere.

"You -- were the man at the lab," she managed, in a brittle, choked voice.

"I'm Leroy Beam. An independent." Awkwardly guiding her, he led her into the kitchen and seated her at the table. She folded her hands in front of her and studied them fixedly; the bleak boniness of her face seemed to be increasing rather than receding. He felt uneasy.

"Are you all right?" he asked.

She nodded.

"Cup of coffee?" He began searching the cupboards for a bottle of Venusian-grown coffee substitute. While he was looking, Ellen Ackers said tautly: "You better go in there. In the bathroom. I don't think he's dead, but he might be."

Beam raced into the bathroom. Behind the plastic shower curtain was an opaque shape. It was Paul Tirol, lying wadded up in the tub, fully clothed. He was not dead but he had been struck behind the left ear and his scalp was leaking a slow, steady trickle of blood. Beam took his pulse, listened to his breathing, and then straightened up.

At the doorway Ellen Ackers materialized, still pale with fright. "Is he? Did I kill him?"

"He's fine."

Visibly, she relaxed. "Thank God. It happened so fast -- he stepped ahead of me to take the *M* inside his place, and then I did it. I hit him as lightly as I could. He was so interested in it. . . he forgot about me." Words spilled from her, quick, jerky sentences, punctuated by rigid tremors of her hands. "I lugged him back in the car and drove here; it was all I could think of."

"What are you in this for?"

Her hysteria rose in a spasm of convulsive muscle-twitching. "It was all planned -- I had *everything* worked out. As soon as I got hold of it I was going to --" She broke off.

"Blackmail Tirol?" he asked, fascinated.

She smiled weakly. "No, not Paul. It was Paul who gave me the idea . . . it was his first idea, when his researchers showed him the thing. The *M,* he calls it. *M* stands for machine. He means it can't be educated, morally corrected."

Incredulous, Beam said: "You were going to blackmail your husband."

Ellen Ackers nodded. "So he'd let me leave."

Suddenly Beam felt sincere respect for her. "My God -- the rattle. Heimie didn't arrange that; *you* did. So the device would be trapped in the apartment."

"Yes," she agreed. "I was going to pick it up. But Paul showed up with other ideas; he wanted it, too."

"What went haywire? You have it, don't you?"

Silently she indicated the linen closet. "I stuffed it away when I heard you."

Beam opened the linen closet. Resting primly on the neatly-folded towels was a small, familiar, portable TV unit.

"It's reverted," Ellen said, from behind him, in an utterly defeated monotone. "As soon as I hit Paul it changed. For half an hour I've been trying to get it to shift. It won't. It'll stay that way forever."

Beam went to the telephone and called a doctor. In the bathroom, Tirol groaned and feebly thrashed his arms. He was beginning to return to consciousness.

"Was that necessary?" Ellen Ackers demanded. "The doctor -- did you have to call?"

Beam ignored her. Bending, he lifted the portable TV unit and held it in his hands; he felt its weight move up his arms like a slow, leaden fatigue. The ultimate adversary, he thought; too stupid to be defeated. It was worse than an animal. It was a rock, solid and dense, lacking all qualities. Except, he thought, the quality of determination. It was determined to persist, to survive; a rock with will. He felt as if he were holding up the universe, and he put the unreconstructed M down.

From behind him Ellen said: "It drives you crazy." Her voice had regained tone. She lit a cigarette with a silver cigarette lighter and then shoved her hands in the pockets of her suit.

"Yes," he said.

"There's nothing you can do, is there? You tried to get it open before. They'll patch Paul up, and he'll go back to his place, and Lantano will be banished --" She took a deep shuddering breath. "And the Interior Department will go on as always."

"Yes," he said. Still kneeling, he surveyed the M. Now, with what he knew, he did not waste time struggling with it. He considered it impassively; he did not even bother to touch it.

In the bathroom, Paul Tirol was trying to crawl from the tub. He slipped back, cursed and moaned, and started his laborious ascent once again.

"Ellen?" his voice quavered, a dim and distorted sound, like dry wires rubbing.

"Take it easy," she said between her teeth; not moving she stood smoking rapidly on her cigarette.

"Help me, Ellen," Tirol muttered. "Something happened to me . . . I don't remember what. Something hit me."

"He'll remember," Ellen said.

Beam said: "I can take this thing to Ackers as it is. You can tell him what it's for -- what it did. That ought to be enough; he won't go through with Lantano."

But he didn't believe it, either. Ackers would have to admit a mistake, a basic mistake, and if he had been wrong to pick up Lantano, he was ruined. And so, in a sense, was the whole system of delineation. It could be fooled; it had been fooled. Ackers was rigid, and he would go right on in a straight line: the hell with Lantano. The hell with abstract justice. Better to preserve cultural continuity and keep society running on an even keel.

"Tirol's equipment," Beam said. "Do you know where it is?"

She shrugged wildly. "What equipment?"

"This thing -- " he jabbed at the M -- "was made somewhere."

"Not here, Tirol didn't make it."

"All right," he said reasonably. They had perhaps six minutes more before the doctor and the emergency medical carrier arrived on rooftop. "Who did make it?"

"The alloy was developed on Bellatrix." She spoke jerkily, word by word. "The rind . . . forms a skin on the outside, a bubble that gets sucked in and out of a reservoir. That's its rind, the TV shape. It sucks it back and becomes the M; it's ready to act."

"What made it?" he repeated.

"A Bellatrix machine tool syndicate . . . a subsidiary of Tirol's organization. They're made to be watchdogs. The big plantations on outplanets use them; they patrol. They get poachers."

Beam said: "Then originally they're not set for one person."

"No."

"Then *who* set this for Heimie? Not a machine tool syndicate."

"That was done here."

He straightened up and lifted the portable TV unit. "Let's go. Take me there, where Tirol had it altered."

For a moment the woman did not respond. Grabbing her arm he hustled her to the door. She gasped and stared at him mutely.

"Come on," he said, pushing her out into the hall. The portable TV unit bumped against the door as he shut it; he held the unit tight and followed after Ellen Ackers.

The town was slatternly and run-down, a few retail stores, fuel station, bars and dance halls. It was two hours' flight from Greater New York and it was called Olum.

"Turn right," Ellen said listlessly. She gazed out at the neon signs and rested her arm on the window sill of the ship.

They flew above warehouses and deserted streets. Lights were few. At an intersection Ellen nodded and he set the ship down on a roof.

Below them was a sagging, fly-specked wooden frame store. A peeling sign was propped up in the window: FULTON BROTHERS locksmiths. With the sign were doorknobs, locks, keys, saws, and spring-wound alarm clocks. Somewhere in the interior of the store a yellow night light burned fitfully.

"This way," Ellen said. She stepped from the ship and made her way down a flight of rickety wooden stairs. Beam laid the portable TV unit on the floor of the ship, locked the doors, and then followed after the woman. Holding onto the railing, he descended to a back porch on which were trash cans and a pile of sodden newspapers tied with string. Ellen was unlocking a door and feeling her way inside.

First he found himself in a musty, cramped storeroom. Pipe and rolls of wire and sheets of metal were heaped everywhere; it was like a junkyard. Next came a narrow corridor and then he was standing in the entrance of a workshop. Ellen reached overhead and groped to find the hanging string of a light. The light clicked on. To the right was a long and littered workbench with a hand grinder at one end, a vise, a keyhole saw; two wooden stools were before the bench and half-assembled machinery was stacked on the floor in no apparent order. The workshop was chaotic, dusty, and archaic. On the wall was a threadbare blue coat hung from a nail: the workcoat of a machinist.

"Here," Ellen said, with bitterness. "This is where Paul had it brought. This outfit is owned by the Tirol organization; this whole slum is part of their holdings."

Beam walked to the bench. "To have altered it," he said, "Tirol must have had a plate of Heimie's neural pattern." He overturned a heap of glass jars; screws and washers poured onto the pitted surface of the bench.

"He got it from Heimie's door," Ellen said. "He had Heimie's lock analyzed and Heimie's pattern inferred from the setting of the tumblers."

"And he had the M opened?"

"There's an old mechanic," Ellen said. "A little dried-up old man; he runs this shop. Patrick Fulton. He installed the bias on the M."

"A bias," Beam said, nodding.

"A bias against killing people. Heimie was the exception, for everybody else it took its protective form. Out in the wilds they would have set it for something else, not a TV unit." She laughed, a sudden ripple close to hysteria. "Yes, that would have looked odd, it sitting out in a forest somewhere, a TV unit. They would have made it into a rock or a stick."

"A rock," Beam said. He could imagine it. The M waiting, covered with moss, waiting for months, years, and then weathered and corroded, finally picking up the presence of a human being. Then the M ceasing to be a rock, becoming, in a quick blur of motion, a box one foot wide and two feet long. An oversized cracker box that started forward --

But there was something missing. "The fakery," he said. "Emitting flakes of paint and hair and tobacco. How did that come in?"

In a brittle voice Ellen said: "The landowner murdered the poacher, and he was culpable in the eyes of the law. So the M left clues. Claw marks. Animal blood. Animal hair."

"God," he said, revolted. "Killed by an animal."

"A bear, a wildcat -- whatever was indigenous, it varied. The predator of the region, a natural death." With her toe she touched a cardboard carton under the workbench. "It's in there, it used to be, anyhow. The neural plate, the transmitter, the discarded parts of the M, the schematics."

The carton had been a shipping container for power packs. Now the packs were gone, and in their place was a carefully-wrapped inner box, sealed against moisture and insect infestation. Beam tore away the metal foil and saw that he had found what he wanted. He gingerly carried the contents out and spread them on the workbench among the soldering irons and drills.

"It's all there," Ellen said, without emotion.

"Maybe," he said, "I can leave you out of this. I can take this and the TV unit to Ackers and try it without your testimony."

"Sure," she said wearily.

"What are you going to do?"

"Well," she said, "I can't go back to Paul, so I guess there's not much I can do."

"The blackmail bit was a mistake," he said.

Her eyes glowed. "Okay."

"If he releases Lantano," Beam said, "he'll be asked to resign. Then he'll probably give you your divorce, it won't be important to him one way or another."

"I --" she began. And then she stopped. Her face seemed to fade, as if the color and texture of her flesh was vanishing from within. She lifted one hand and half-turned, her mouth open and the sentence still unfinished.

Beam, reaching, slapped the overhead light out; the workroom winked into darkness. He had heard it too, had heard it at the same time as Ellen Ackers. The rickety outside porch had creaked and now the slow, ponderous motion was past the storeroom and into the hall.

A heavy man, he thought. A slow-moving man, sleepy, making his way step by step, his eyes almost shut, his great body sagging beneath his suit. Beneath, he thought, his expensive tweed suit. In the darkness the man's shape was looming; Beam could not see it but he could sense it there, filling up the doorway as it halted. Boards creaked under its weight. In a daze he wondered if Ackers already knew, if his order had already been rescinded. Or had the man got out on his own, worked through his own organization?

The man, starting forward again, spoke in a deep, husky voice. "Ugh," Lantano said. "Damn it."

Ellen began to shriek. Beam still did not realize what it was; he was still fumbling for the light and wondering stupidly why it did not come on. He had smashed the bulb, he realized. He lit a match; the match went out and he grabbed for Ellen Ackers' cigarette lighter. It was in her purse, and it took him an agonized second to get it out.

The unreconstructed M was approaching them slowly, one receptor stalk extended. Again it halted, swiveled to the left until it was facing the workbench. It was not now in the shape of a portable TV unit; it had retaken its cracker-box shape.

"The plate," Ellen Ackers whispered. "It responded to the plate."

The M had been roused by Heimie Rosenburg's looking for it. But Beam still felt the presence of David Lantano. The big man was still here in the room; the sense of heaviness, the proximity of weight and ponderousness had arrived with the machine, as it moved, sketching Lantano's existence. As he fixedly watched, the machine produced a fragment of cloth fabric and pressed it into a nearby heap of grid-mesh. Other elements, blood and tobacco and hair, were being produced, but they were too small for him to see. The machine pressed a heel mark into the dust of the floor and then projected a nozzle from its anterior section.

Her arm over her eyes, Ellen Ackers ran away. But the machine was not interested in her; revolving in the direction of the workbench it raised itself and fired. An explosive pellet, released by the nozzle, traveled across the workbench and entered the debris heaped across the bench. The pellet detonated; bits of wire and nails showered in particles.

Heimie's dead, Beam thought, and went on watching. The machine was searching for the plate, trying to locate and destroy the synthetic neural emission. It swiveled, lowered its nozzle hesitantly, and then fired again. Behind the workbench, the wall burst and settled into itself.

Beam, holding the cigarette lighter, walked toward the M. A receptor stalk waved toward him and the machine retreated. Its lines wavered, flowed, and then painfully reformed. For an interval, the device struggled with itself; then, reluctantly, the portable TV unit again became visible. From the machine a high-pitched whine emerged, an anguished squeal. Conflicting stimuli were present; the machine was unable to make a decision.

The machine was developing a situation neurosis and the ambivalence of its response was destroying it. In a way its anguish had a human quality, but he could not feel sorry for it. It was a mechanical contraption trying to assume a posture of disguise and attack at the same time; the breakdown was one of relays and tubes, not of a living brain. And it had been a living brain into which it had fired its original pellet. Heimie Rosenburg was dead, and there were no more like him and no possibility that more could be assembled. He went over to the machine and nudged it onto its back with his foot.

The machine whirred snake-like and spun away. "Ugh, damn it!" it said. It showered bits of tobacco as it rolled off; drops of blood and flakes of blue enamel fell from it as it disappeared into the corridor. Beam could hear it moving about, bumping into the walls like a blind, damaged organism. After a moment he followed after it.

In the corridor, the machine was traveling in a slow circle. It was erecting around itself a wall of particles: cloth and hairs and burnt matches and bits of tobacco, the mass cemented together with blood.

"Ugh, damn it," the machine said in its heavy masculine voice. It went on working, and Beam returned to the other room.

"Where's a phone?" he said to Ellen Ackers.

She stared at him vacantly.

"It won't hurt you," he said. He felt dull and worn-out. "It's in a closed cycle. It'll go on until it runs down."

"It went crazy," she said. She shuddered.

"No," he said. "Regression. It's trying to hide."

From the corridor the machine said, "Ugh. Damn it." Beam found the phone and called Edward Ackers.

Banishment for Paul Tirol meant first a procession of bands of darkness and then a protracted, infuriating interval in which empty matter drifted randomly around him, arranging itself into first one pattern and then another.

The period between the time Ellen Ackers attacked him and the time banishment sentence had been pronounced was vague and dim in his mind. Like the present shadows, it was hard to pin down.

He had -- he thought -- awakened in Ackers' apartment. Yes, that was it; and Leroy Beam was there, too. A sort of transcendental Leroy Beam who hovered robustly around, arranging everybody in configurations of his choice. A doctor had come. And finally Edward Ackers had shown up to face his wife and the situation.

Bandaged, and on his way into Interior, he had caught a glimpse of a man going out. The ponderous, bulbous shape of David Lantano, on his way home to his luxurious stone mansion and acre of grass.

At sight of him Tirol had felt a goad of fear. Lantano hadn't even noticed him; an acutely thoughtful expression on his face, Lantano padded into a waiting car and departed.

"You have one thousand dollars," Edward Ackers was saying wearily, during the final phase. Distorted, Ackers' face bloomed again in the drifting shadows around Tirol, an image of the man's last appearance. Ackers, too, was ruined, but in a different way. "The law supplies you with one thousand dollars to meet your immediate needs, also you'll find a pocket dictionary of representative out-system dialects."

Ionization itself was painless. He had no memory of it; only a blank space darker than the blurred images on either side.

"You hate me," he had declared accusingly, his last words to Ackers. "I destroyed you. But. . . it wasn't you." He had been confused. "Lantano. Maneuvered but not. How? You did . . ."

But Lantano had had nothing to do with it. Lantano had shambled off home, a withdrawn spectator throughout. The hell with Lantano. The hell with Ackers and Leroy Beam and -- reluctantly -- the hell with Mrs. Ellen Ackers.

"Wow," Tirol babbled, as his drifting body finally collected physical shape. "We had a lot of good times . . . didn't we, Ellen?"

And then a roaring hot field of sunlight was radiating down on him. Stupefied, he sat slumped over, limp and passive. Yellow, scalding sunlight. . . everywhere. Nothing but the dancing heat of it, blinding him, cowing him into submission.

He was sprawled in the middle of a yellow clay road. To his right was a baking, drying field of corn wilted in the midday heat. A pair of large, disreputable-looking birds wheeled silently overhead. A long way off was a line of blunted hills: ragged troughs and peaks that seemed nothing more than heaps of dust. At their base was a meager lump of man-made buildings.

At least he *hoped* they were man-made.

As he climbed shakily to his feet, a feeble noise drifted to his ears. Coming down the hot, dirty road was a car of some sort. Apprehensive and cautious, Tirol walked to meet it.

The driver was human, a thin, almost emaciated youth with pebbled black skin and a heavy mass of weed-colored hair. He wore a stained canvas shirt and overalls. A bent, unlit cigarette hung from his lower lip. The car was a combustion-driven model and had rolled out of the twentieth century; battered and twisted, it rattled to a halt as the driver critically inspected Tirol. From the car's radio yammered a torrent of tinny dance music.

"You a tax collector?" the driver asked.

"Certainly not," Tirol said, knowing the bucolic hostility toward tax collectors. But -- he floundered. He couldn't confess that he was a banished criminal from Earth; that was an invitation to be massacred, usually in some picturesque way. "I'm an inspector," he announced, "Department of Health."

Satisfied, the driver nodded. "Lots of scuttly cutbeede, these days. You fellows got a spray, yet? Losing one crop after another."

Tirol gratefully climbed into the car. "I didn't realize the sun was so hot," he murmured.

"You've got an accent," the youth observed, starting up the engine. "Where you from?"

"Speech impediment," Tirol said cagily. "How long before we reach town?"

"Oh, maybe an hour," the youth answered, as the car wandered lazily forward.

Tirol was afraid to ask the name of the planet. It would give him away. But he was consumed with the need to know. He might be two star-systems away or two million; he might be a month out of Earth or seventy years. Naturally, he had to get back; he had no intention of becoming a sharecropper on some backwater colony planet.

"Pretty swip," the youth said, indicating the torrent of noxious jazz pouring from the car radio. "That's Calamine Freddy and his Woolybear Creole Original Band. Know that tune?"

"No," Tirol muttered. The sun and dryness and heat made his head ache, and he wished to God he knew where he was.

The town was miserably tiny. The houses were dilapidated; the streets were dirt. A kind of domestic chicken roamed here and there, pecking in the rubbish. Under a porch a bluish quasi-dog lay sleeping. Perspiring and unhappy, Paul Tirol entered the bus station and located a schedule. A series of meaningless entries flashed by: names of towns. The name of the planet, of course, was not listed.

"What's the fare to the nearest port?" he asked the indolent official behind the ticket window.

The official considered. "Depends on what sort of port you want. Where you planning to go?"

"Toward Center," Tirol said. "Center" was the term used in out-systems for the Sol Group.

Dispassionately, the official shook his head. "No inter-system port around here."

Tirol was baffled. Evidently, he wasn't on the hub planet of this particular system. "Well," he said, "then the nearest interplan port."

The official consulted a vast reference book. "You want to go to which system-member?"

"Whichever one has the inter-system port," Tirol said patiently. He would leave from there. "That would be Venus."

Astonished, Tirol said: "Then this system -- " He broke off, chagrined, as he remembered. It was the parochial custom in many out-systems, especially those a long way out, to name their member planets after the original nine. This one was probably called "Mars" or "Jupiter" or "Earth," depending on its position in the group. "Fine," Tirol finished. "One-way ticket to -- Venus."

Venus, or what passed for Venus, was a dismal orb no larger than an asteroid. A bleak cloud of metallic haze hung over it, obscuring the sun. Except for mining and smelting operations the planet was deserted. A few dreary shacks dotted the barren countryside. A perpetual wind blew, scattering debris and trash.

But the inter-system port was here, the field which linked the planet to its nearest star-neighbor and, ultimately, with the balance of the universe. At the moment a giant freighter was taking ore.

Tirol entered the ticket office. Spreading out most of his remaining money he said: "I want a one-way ticket taking me toward Center. As far as I can go."

The clerk calculated. "You care what class?"

"No," he said, mopping his forehead.

"How fast?"

"No."

The clerk said: "That'll carry you as far as the Betelgeuse System."

"Good enough," Tirol said, wondering what he did then. But at least he could contact his organization from there; he was already back in the charted universe. But now he was almost broke. He felt a prickle of icy fear, despite the heat.

The hub planet of the Betelgeuse System was called Plantagenet III. It was a thriving junction for passenger carriers transporting settlers to undeveloped colony planets. As soon as Tirol's ship landed he hurried across the field to the taxi stand.

"Take me to Tirol Enterprises," he instructed, praying there was an outlet here. There had to be, but it might be operating under a front name. Years ago he lost track of the particulars of his sprawling empire.

"Tirol Enterprises," the cab driver repeated thoughtfully. "Nope, no such outfit, mister."

Stunned, Tirol said: "Who does the slaving around here?"

The driver eyed him. He was a wizened, dried-up little man with glasses; he peered turtle-wise, without compassion. "Well," he said, "I've been told you can get carried out-system without papers. There's a shipping contractor. . . called --" He reflected. Tirol, trembling, handed him a last bill.

"The Reliable Export-Import," the driver said.

That was one of Lantano's fronts. In horror Tirol said: "And that's it?"

The driver nodded.

Dazed, Tirol moved away from the cab. The buildings of the field danced around him; he settled down on a bench to catch his breath. Under his coat his heart pounded unevenly. He tried to breathe, but his breath caught painfully in his throat. The bruise on his head where Ellen Ackers had hit him began to throb. It was true, and he was gradually beginning to understand and believe it. He was not going to get to Earth; he was going to spend the rest of his life here on this rural world, cut off from his organization and everything he had built up over the years.

And, he realized, as he sat struggling to breathe, the rest of his life was not going to be very long.

He thought about Heimie Rosenburg.

"Betrayed," he said, and coughed wrackingly. "You betrayed me. You hear that? Because of you I'm here. It's your fault; I never should have hired you."

He thought about Ellen Ackers. "You too," he gasped, coughing. Sitting on the bench he alternately coughed and gasped and thought about the people who had betrayed him. There were hundreds of them.

The living room of David Lantano's house was furnished in exquisite taste. Priceless late nineteenth century Blue Willow dishes lined the walls in a rack of wrought iron. At his antique yellow plastic and chrome table, David Lantano was eating dinner, and the spread of food amazed Beam even more than the house.

Lantano was in good humor and he ate with enthusiasm. His linen napkin was tucked under his chin and once, as he sipped coffee, he dribbled and belched. His brief period of confinement was over; he ate to make up for the ordeal.

He had been informed, first by his own apparatus and now by Beam, that banishment had successfully carried Tirol past the point of return. Tirol would not be coming back and for that Lantano was thankful. He felt expansive toward Beam; he wished Beam would have something to eat.

Moodily, Beam said: "It's nice here."

"You could have something like this," Lantano said.

On the wall hung a framed folio of ancient paper protected by helium-filled glass. It was the first printing of a poem of Ogden Nash, a collector's item that should have been in a museum. It aroused in Beam a mixed feeling of longing and aversion.

"Yes," Beam said. "I could have this." This, he thought, or Ellen Ackers or the job at Interior or perhaps all three at once. Edward Ackers had been retired on pension and he had given his wife a divorce. Lantano was out of jeopardy. Tirol had been banished. He wondered what he did want.

"You could go a long way," Lantano said sleepily.

"As far as Paul Tirol?"

Lantano chuckled and yawned.

"I wonder if he left any family," Beam said. "Any children." He was thinking about Heimie.

Lantano reached across the table toward the bowl of fruit. He selected a peach and carefully brushed it against the sleeve of his robe. "Try a peach," he said.

"No thanks," Beam said irritably.

Lantano examined the peach but he did not eat it. The peach was made of wax; the fruit in the bowl was imitation. He was not really as rich as he pretended, and many of the artifacts about the living room were fakes. Each time he offered fruit to a visitor he took a calculated risk. Returning the peach to the bowl he leaned back in his chair and sipped his coffee.

If Beam did not have plans, at least *he* had, and with Tirol gone the plans had a better than even chance of working out. He felt peaceful. Someday, he thought, and not too far off, the fruit in the bowl would be real.

Breakfast at Twilight

"Dad?" Earl asked, hurrying out of the bathroom, "you going to drive us to school today?"

Tim McLean poured himself a second cup of coffee. "You kids can walk for a change. The car's in the garage."

Judy pouted. "It's raining."

"No it isn't," Virginia corrected her sister. She drew the shade back. "It's all foggy, but it isn't raining."

"Let me look." Mary McLean dried her hands and came over from the sink. "What an odd day. Is that fog? It looks more like smoke. I can't make out a thing. What did the weatherman say?"

"I couldn't get anything on the radio," Earl said. "Nothing but static."

Tim stirred angrily. "That darn thing on the blink again? Seems like I just had it fixed." He got up and moved sleepily over to the radio. He fiddled idly with the dials. The three children hurried back and forth, getting ready for school. "Strange," Tim said.

"I'm going." Earl opened the front door.

"Wait for your sisters," Mary ordered absently.

"I'm ready," Virginia said. "Do I look all right?"

"You look fine," Mary said, kissing her.

"I'll call the radio repair place from the office," Tim said.

He broke off. Earl stood at the kitchen door, pale and silent, his eyes wide with terror.

"What is it?"

"I -- I came back."

"What is it? Are you sick?"

"I can't go to school."

They stared at him. "What is wrong?" Tim grabbed his son's arm. "Why can't you go to school?"

"They -- they won't let me."

"Who?"

"The soldiers." It came tumbling out with a rush. "They're all over. Soldiers and guns. And they're coming here."

"Coming? Coming here?" Tim echoed, dazed.

"They're coming here and they're going to --" Earl broke off, terrified. From the front porch came the sound of heavy boots. A crash. Splintering wood. Voices.

"Good Lord," Mary gasped. "What is it, Tim?"

Tim entered the living-room, his heart laboring painfully. Three men stood inside the door. Men in gray-green uniforms, weighted with guns and complex tangles of equipment. Tubes and hoses. Meters on thick cords. Boxes and leather straps and antennae. Elaborate masks locked over their heads. Behind the masks Tim saw tired, whisker-stubbled faces, red-rimmed eyes that gazed at him in brutal displeasure.

One of the soldiers jerked up his gun, aiming at McLean's middle. Tim peered at it dumbly. *The gun.* Long and thin. Like a needle. Attached to a coil of tubes.

"What in the name of --" he began, but the soldier cut him off savagely.

"Who are you?" His voice was harsh, guttural. "What are you doing here?" He pushed his mask aside. His skin was dirty. Cuts and pocks lined his sallow flesh. His teeth were broken and missing.

"Answer!" a second soldier demanded. "What are you doing here?"

"Show your blue card," the third said. "Let's see your Sector number." His eyes strayed to the children and Mary standing mutely at the dining-room door. His mouth fell open.

"A woman?"

The three soldiers gazed in disbelief.

"What the hell is this?" the first demanded. "How long has this woman been here?"

Tim found his voice. "She's my wife. What is this? What --"

"Your *wife?*" They were incredulous.

"My wife and children. For God's sake --"

"Your wife? And you'd bring her here? You must be out of your head!"

"He's got ash sickness," one said. He lowered his gun and strode across the living-room to Mary. "Come on, sister. You're coming with us."

Tim lunged.

A wall of force hit him. He sprawled, clouds of darkness rolling around him. His ears sang. His head throbbed. Everything receded. Dimly, he was aware of shapes moving. Voices. The room. He concentrated.

The soldiers were herding the children back. One of them grabbed Mary by the arm. He tore her dress away, ripping it from her shoulders. "Gee," he snarled. "He'd bring her here, and she's not even strung!"

"Take her along."

"Okay, Captain." The soldier dragged Mary toward the front door. "We'll do what we can with her."

"The kids." The captain waved the other soldier over with the children. "Take them along. I don't get it. No masks. No cards. How'd this house miss getting hit? Last night was the worst in months!"

Tim struggled painfully to his feet. His mouth was bleeding. His vision blurred. He hung on tight to the wall. "Look," he muttered. "For God's sake --"

The captain was staring into the kitchen. "Is that -- is that *food?*" He advanced slowly through the dining-room. "Look!"

The other soldiers came after him, Mary and the children forgotten. They stood around the table, amazed.

"Look at it!"

"Coffee." One grabbed up the pot and drank it greedily down. He choked, black coffee dripping down his tunic. "Hot. Jeez. Hot coffee."

"Cream!" Another soldier tore open the refrigerator. "Look. Milk. Eggs. Butter. Meat." His voice broke. "It's full of food."

The captain disappeared into the pantry. He came out, lugging a case of canned peas. "Get the rest. Get it all. We'll load it in the snake."

He dropped the case on the table with a crash. Watching Tim intently, he fumbled in his dirty tunic until he found a cigarette.

He lit it slowly, not taking his eyes from Tim. "All right," he said. "Let's hear what you have to say."

Tim's mouth opened and closed. No words came. His mind was blank. Dead. He couldn't think.

"This food. Where'd you get it? And these things." The captain waved around the kitchen. "Dishes. Furniture. How come this house hasn't been hit? How did you survive last night's attack?"

"I --" Tim gasped.

The captain came toward him ominously. "The woman. And the kids. All of you. What are you doing here?" His voice was hard. "You better be able to explain, mister. You better be able to explain what you're doing here -- or we'll have to burn the whole damn lot of you."

Tim sat down at the table. He took a deep, shuddering breath, trying to focus his mind. His body ached. He rubbed blood from his mouth, conscious of a broken molar and bits of loose tooth. He got out a handkerchief and spat the bits into it. His hands were shaking.

"Come on," the captain said.

Mary and the children slipped into the room. Judy was crying. Virginia's face was blank with shock. Earl stared wide-eyed at the soldiers, his face white.

"Tim," Mary said, putting her hand on his arm. "Are you all right?"

Tim nodded. "I'm all right."

Mary pulled her dress around her. "Tim, they can't get away with it. Somebody'll come. The mailman. The neighbors. They can't just --"

"Shut up," the captain snapped. His eyes flickered oddly. "The mailman? What are you talking about?" He held out his hand. "Let's see your yellow slip, sister."

"Yellow slip?" Mary faltered.

The captain rubbed his jaw. "No yellow slip. No masks. No cards."

"They're geeps," a soldier said.

"Maybe. And maybe not."

"They're geeps, Captain. We better burn 'em. We can't take any chances."

"There's something funny going on here," the captain said. He plucked at his neck, lifting up a small box on a cord. "I'm getting a polic here."

"A polic?" A shiver moved through the soldiers. "Wait, Captain. We can handle this. Don't get a polic. He'll put us on 4 and then we'll never --"

The captain spoke into the box. "Give me Web B."

Tim looked up at Mary. "Listen, honey. I --"

"Shut up." A soldier prodded him. Tim lapsed into silence.

The box squawked. "Web B."

"Can you spare a polic? We've run into something strange. Group of five. Man, woman, three kids. No masks, no cards, the woman not strung, dwelling completely intact. Furniture, fixtures, about two hundred pounds of food."

The box hesitated. "All right. Polic on the way. Stay there. Don't let them escape."

"I won't." The captain dropped the box back in his shirt. "A polic will be here any minute. Meanwhile, let's get the food loaded."

From outside came a deep thundering roar. It shook the house, rattling the dishes in the cupboard.

"Jeez," a soldier said. That was close."

"I hope the screens hold until nightfall." The captain grabbed up the case of canned peas. "Get the rest. We want it loaded before the polic comes."

The two soldiers filled their arms and followed him through the house, out the front door. Their voices diminished as they strode down the path.

Tim got to his feet. "Stay here," he said thickly.

"What are you doing?" Mary asked nervously.

"Maybe I can get out." He ran to the back door and unlatched it, hands shaking. He pulled the door wide and stepped out on the back porch. "I don't see any of them. If we can only. . ."

He stopped.

Around him gray clouds blew. Gray ash, billowing as far as he could see. Dim shapes were visible. Broken shapes, silent and unmoving in the grayness.

Ruins.

Ruined buildings. Heaps of rubble. Debris everywhere. He walked slowly down the back steps. The concrete walk ended abruptly. Beyond it, slag and heaps of rubble were strewn. Nothing else. Nothing as far as the eye could see.

Nothing stirred. Nothing moved. In the gray silence there was no life. No motion. Only the clouds of drifting ash. The slag and the endless heaps.

The city was gone. The buildings were destroyed. Nothing remained. No people. No life. Jagged walls, empty and gaping. A few dark weeds growing among the debris. Tim bent down, touching a weed. Rough, thick stalk. And the slag. It was a metal slag. Melted metal. He straightened up --

"Come back inside," a crisp voice said.

He turned numbly. A man stood on the porch, behind him, hands on his hips. A small man, hollow-cheeked. Eyes small and bright, like two black coals. He wore a uniform different from the soldiers'. His mask was pushed back, away from his face. His skin was yellow, faintly luminous, clinging to his cheekbones. A sick face, ravaged by fever and fatigue.

"Who are you?" Tim said.

"Douglas. Political Commissioner Douglas."

"You're -- you're the police," Tim said.

"That's right. Now come inside. I expect to hear some answers from you. I have quite a few questions."

"The first thing I want to know," Commissioner Douglas said, "is how this house escaped destruction."

Tim and Mary and the children sat together on the couch, silent and unmoving, faces blank with shock.

"Well?" Douglas demanded.

Tim found his voice. "Look," he said. "I don't know. I don't know anything. We woke up this morning like every other morning. We dressed and ate breakfast --"

"It was foggy out," Virginia said. "We looked out and saw the fog."

"And the radio wouldn't work," Earl said.

"The radio?" Douglas's thin face twisted. "There haven't been any audio signals in months. Except for government purposes. This house. All of you. I don't understand. If you were geeps --"

"Geeps. What does that mean?" Mary murmured.

"Soviet general-purpose troops."

"Then the war has begun."

"North America was attacked two years ago," Douglas said. "In 1978."

Tim sagged. "1978. Then this is 1980." He reached suddenly into his pocket. He pulled out his wallet and tossed it to Douglas. "Look in there."

Douglas opened the wallet suspiciously. "Why?"

"The library card. The parcel receipts. Look at the dates." Tim turned to Mary. "I'm beginning to understand now. I had an idea when I saw the ruins."

"Are we winning?" Earl piped.

Douglas studied Tim's wallet intently. "Very interesting. These are all old. Seven and eight years." His eyes flickered. "What are you trying to say? That you came from the past? That you're time travelers?"

The captain came back inside. "The snake is all loaded, sir."

Douglas nodded curtly. "All right. You can take off with your patrol."

The captain glanced at Tim. "Will you be --"

"I'll handle them."

The captain saluted. "Fine, sir." He quickly disappeared through the door. Outside, he and his men climbed aboard a long thin truck, like a pipe mounted on treads. With a faint hum the truck leaped forward.

In a moment only gray clouds and the dim outline of ruined buildings remained.

Douglas paced back and forth, examining the living-room, the wallpaper, the light fixture and chairs. He picked up some magazines and thumbed through them. "From the past. But not far in the past."

"Seven years?"

"Could it be? I suppose. A lot of things have happened in the last few months. Time travel." Douglas grinned ironically. "You picked a bad spot, McLean. You should have gone farther on."

"I didn't pick it. It just happened."

"You must have done *something*."

Tim shook his head. "No. Nothing. We got up. And we were -- here."

Douglas was deep in thought. "Here. Seven years in the future. Moved forward through time. We know nothing about time travel. No work has been done with it. There seem to be evident military possibilities."

"How did the war begin?" Mary asked faintly.

"Begin? It didn't begin. You remember. There was war seven years ago."

"The real war. This."

"There wasn't any point when it became -- this. We fought in Korea. We fought in China. In Germany and Yugoslavia and Iran. It spread, farther and farther. Finally the bombs were falling here. It came like the plague. The war *grew*. It didn't begin." Abruptly he put his notebook away. "A report on you would be suspect. They might think that I had the ash sickness."

"What's that?" Virginia asked.

"Radioactive particles in the air. Carried to the brain. Causes insanity. Everybody has a touch of it, even with the masks."

"I'd sure like to know who's winning," Earl repeated. "What was that outside? That truck. Was it rocket propelled?"

"The snake? No. Turbines. Boring snout. Cuts through the debris."

"Seven years," Mary said. "So much has changed. It doesn't seem possible."

"So much?" Douglas shrugged. "I suppose so. I remember what I was doing seven years ago. I was still in school. Learning. I had an apartment and a car. I went out dancing. I bought a TV set. But these things were there. The twilight. This. Only I didn't know. None of us knew. But they were there."

"You're a Political Commissioner?" Tim asked.

"I supervise the troops. Watch for political deviation. In a total war we have to keep people under constant surveillance. One Commie down in the Webs could wreck the whole business. We can't take chances."

Tim nodded. "Yes. It was there. The twilight. Only we didn't understand it."

Douglas examined the books in the bookcase. "I'll take a couple of these along. I haven't seen fiction in months. Most of it disappeared. Burned back in '77."

"Burned?"

Douglas helped himself. "Shakespeare. Milton. Dryden. I'll take the old stuff. It's safer. None of the Steinbeck and Dos Passos. Even a polic can get in trouble. If you stay here, you better get rid of *that*." He tapped a volume of Dostoevski, *The Brothers Karamazov*.

"If we stay! What else can we do?"

"You want to stay?"

"No," Mary said quietly.

Douglas shot her a quick glance. "No, I suppose not. If you stay you'll be separated, of course. Children to the Canadian Relocation Centers. Women are situated down in the under-surface factory-labor camps. Men are automatically a part of Military."

"Like those there who left," Tim said.

"Unless you can qualify for the id block."

"What's that?"

"Industrial Designing and Technology. What training have you had? Anything along scientific lines?"

"No. Accounting."

Douglas shrugged. "Well, you'll be given a standard test. If your IQ is high enough you could go in the Political Service. We use a lot of men." He paused thoughtfully, his arms loaded with books. "You better go back, McLean. You'll have trouble getting accustomed to this. I'd go back, if I could. But I can't."

"Back?" Mary echoed. "How?"

"The way you came."

"We just came."

Douglas halted at the front door. "Last night was the worst rom attack so far. They hit this whole area."

"Rom?"

"Robot operated missiles. The Soviets are systematically destroying continental America, mile by mile. Roms are cheap. They make them by the million and fire them off. The whole process is automatic. Robot factories turn them out and fire them at us. Last night they came over here -- waves of them. This morning the patrol came in and found nothing. Except you, of course."

Tim nodded slowly. "I'm beginning to see."

"The concentrated energy must have tipped some unstable time fault. Like a rock fault. We're always starting earthquakes. But a *time quake*. . . Interesting. That's what happened, I think. The release of energy, the destruction of matter, sucked your house into the future. Carried the house seven years ahead. This street, everything here, this very spot, was pulverized. Your house, seven years back, was caught in the undertow. The blast must have lashed back through time."

"Sucked into the future," Tim said. "During the night. While we were asleep."

Douglas watched him carefully. "Tonight," he said, "there will be another rom attack. It should finish off what is left." He looked at his watch. "It is now four in the afternoon. The attack will begin in a few hours. You should be undersurface. Nothing will survive up here. I can take you down with me, if you want. But if you want to take a chance, if you want to stay here --"

"You think it might tip us back?"

"Maybe. I don't know. It's a gamble. It might tip you back to your own time, or it might not. If not --"

"If not we wouldn't have a chance of survival."

Douglas flicked out a pocket map and spread it open on the couch. "A patrol will remain in this area another half-hour. If you decide to come undersurface with us, go down the street this way." He traced a line on the map. "To this open field here. The patrol is a Political unit. They'll take you the rest of the way down. You think you can find the field?"

"I think so," Tim said, looking at the map. His lips twisted. "That open field used to be the grammar school my kids went to. That's where they were going when the troops stopped them. Just a little while ago."

"Seven years ago," Douglas corrected. He snapped the map shut and restored it to his pocket. He pulled his mask down and moved out the front door onto the porch. "Maybe I'll see you again. Maybe not. It's your decision. You'll have to decide one way or the other. In any case -- good luck."

He turned and walked briskly from the house.

"Dad," Earl shouted, "are you going in the Army? Are you going to wear a mask and shoot one of those guns?" His eyes sparkled with excitement. "Are you going to drive a *snake?*"

Tim McLean squatted down and pulled his son to him. "You want that? *You want to stay here?* If I'm going to wear a mask and shoot one of those guns we can't go back."

Earl looked doubtful. "Couldn't we go back later?"

Tim shook his head. "Afraid not. We've got to decide now, whether we're going back or not."

"You heard Mr Douglas," Virginia said disgustedly. "The attack's going to start in a couple hours."

Tim got to his feet and paced back and forth. "If we stay in the house we'll get blown to bits. Let's face it. There's only a faint chance we'll be tipped back to our own time. A slim possibility -- a long shot. Do we want to stay here with roms falling all around us, knowing any second it may be the end -- hearing them come closer, hitting nearer -- lying on the floor, waiting, listening --"

"Do you really want to go back?" Mary demanded.

"Of course, but the risk --"

"I'm not asking you about the risk. I'm asking you if you really want to go back. Maybe you want to stay here. Maybe Earl's right. You in a uniform and a mask, with one of those needle guns. Driving a snake."

"With you in a factory-labor camp! And the kids in a Government Relocation Center! How do you think that would be? What do you think they'd teach them? What do you think they'd grow up like? And believe. . ."

"They'd probably teach them to be very useful."

"Useful! To what? To themselves? To mankind? Or to the war effort. . .?"

"They'd be alive," Mary said. "They'd be safe. This way, if we stay in the house, wait for the attack to come --"

"Sure," Tim grated. "They would be alive. Probably quite healthy. Well fed. Well clothed and cared for." He looked down at his children, his face hard. "They'd stay alive, all right. They'd live to grow up and become adults. But what kind of adults? You heard what he said! Book burnings in '77. What'll they be taught from? What kind of ideas are left, since '77? What kind of beliefs can they get from a Government Relocation Center? What kind of values will they have?"

"There's the id block," Mary suggested.

"Industrial Designing and Technology. For the bright ones. The clever ones with imagination. Busy slide rules and pencils. Drawing and planning and making discoveries. The girls could go into that. They could design the guns. Earl could go into the Political Service. He could make sure the guns were used. If any of the troops deviated, didn't want to shoot, Earl could report them and have them hauled off for reeducation. To have their political faith strengthened -- in a world where those *with* brains design weapons and those *without* brains fire them."

"But they'd be alive," Mary repeated.

"You've got a strange idea of what being alive is! You call that alive? Maybe it is." Tim shook his head wearily. "Maybe you're right. Maybe we should go undersurface with Douglas. Stay in this world. Stay alive."

"I didn't say that," Mary said softly. "Tim, I had to find out if you *really* understood why it's worth it. Worth staying in the house, taking the chance we won't be tipped back."

"Then you want to take the chance?"

"Of course! We *have* to. We can't turn our children over to them -- to the Relocation Center. To be taught how to hate and kill and destroy." Mary smiled up wanly. "Anyhow, they've always gone to the Jefferson School. And here, in this world, it's only an open field."

"Are we going back?" Judy piped. She caught hold of Tim's sleeve imploringly. "Are we going back now?"

Tim disengaged her arm. "Very soon, honey."

Mary opened the supply cupboards and rooted in them. "Everything's here. What did they take?"

"The case of canned peas. Everything we had in the refrigerator. And they smashed the front door."

"I'll bet we're beating them!" Earl shouted. He ran to the window and peered out. The sight of the rolling ash disappointed him. "I can't see anything! Just the fog!" He turned questioningly to Tim. "Is it always like this, here?"

"Yes," Tim answered.

Earl's face fell. "Just fog? Nothing else. Doesn't the sun shine ever?"

"I'll fix some coffee," Mary said.

"Good." Tim went into the bathroom and examined himself in the mirror. His mouth was cut, caked with dried blood. His head ached. He felt sick at his stomach.

"It doesn't seem possible," Mary said, as they sat down at the kitchen table.

Tim sipped his coffee. "No. It doesn't." Where he sat he could see out the window. The clouds of ash. The dim, jagged outline of ruined buildings.

"Is the man coming back?" Judy piped. "He was all thin and funny-looking. He isn't coming back, is he?"

Tim looked at his watch. It read ten o'clock. He reset it, moving the hands to four-fifteen. "Douglas said it would begin at nightfall. That won't be long."

"Then we're really staying in the house," Mary said.

"That's right."

"Even though there's only a little chance?"

"Even though there's only a little chance we'll get back. Are you glad?"

"I'm glad," Mary said, her eyes bright. "It's worth it, Tim. You know it is. Anything's worth it, any chance. *To get back.* And something else. We'll all be here together. . . We can't be -- broken up. Separated."

Tim poured himself more coffee. "We might as well make ourselves comfortable. We have maybe three hours to wait. We might as well try to enjoy them."

At six-thirty the first rom fell. They felt the shock, a deep rolling wave of force that lapped over the house.

Judy came running in from the dining-room, face white with fear. "Daddy! What is it?"

"Nothing. Don't worry."

"Come on back," Virginia called impatiently. "It's your turn." They were playing Monopoly.

Earl leaped to his feet. "I want to see." He ran excitedly to the window. "I can see where it hit!"

Tim lifted the shade and looked out. Far off, in the distance, a white glare burned fitfully. A towering column of luminous smoke rose from it.

A second shudder vibrated through the house. A dish crashed from the shelf, into the sink.

It was almost dark outside. Except for the two spots of white Tim could make out nothing. The clouds of ash were lost in the gloom. The ash and the ragged remains of buildings.

"That was closer," Mary said.

A third rom fell. In the living-room windows burst, showering glass across the rug.

"We better get back," Tim said.

"Where?"

"Down in the basement. Come on." Tim unlocked the basement door and they trooped nervously downstairs.

"Food," Mary said. "We better bring the food that's left."

"Good idea. You kids go on down. We'll come along in a minute."

"I can carry something," Earl said.

"Go on down." The fourth rom hit, farther off than the last. "And stay away from the window."

"I'll move something over the window," Earl said. "The big piece of plywood we used for my train."

"Good idea." Tim and Mary returned to the kitchen. "Food. Dishes. What else?"

"Books." Mary looked nervously around. "I don't know. Nothing else. Come on."

A shattering roar drowned out her words. The kitchen window gave, showering glass over them. The dishes over the sink tumbled down in a torrent of breaking china. Tim grabbed Mary and pulled her down.

From the broken window rolling clouds of ominous gray drifted into the room. The evening air stank, a sour, rotten smell. Tim shuddered.

"Forget the food. Let's get back down."

"But --"

"Forget it." He grabbed her and pulled her down the basement stairs. They tumbled in a heap, Tim slamming the door after them.

"Where's the food?" Virginia demanded.

Tim wiped his forehead shakily. "Forget it. We won't need it."

"Help me," Earl gasped. Tim helped him move the sheet of plywood over the window above the laundry tubs. The basement was cold and silent. The cement floor under them was faintly moist.

Two roms struck at once. Tim was hurled to the floor. The concrete hit him and he grunted. For a moment blackness swirled around him. Then he was on his knees, groping his way up.

"Everybody all right?" he muttered.

"I'm all right," Mary said. Judy began to whimper. Earl was feeling his way across the room.

"I'm all right," Virginia said. "I guess."

The lights flickered and dimmed. Abruptly they went out. The basement was pitch-black.

"Well," Tim said. "There they go."

"I have my flashlight." Earl winked the flashlight on. "How's that?"

"Fine," Tim said.

More roms hit. The ground leaped under them, bucking and heaving. A wave of force shuddering the whole house.

"We better lie down," Mary said.

"Yes. Lie down." Tim stretched himself out awkwardly. A few bits of plaster rained down around them.

"When will it stop?" Earl asked uneasily.

"Soon," Tim said.

"Then we'll be back?"

"Yes. We'll be back."

The next blast hit them almost at once. Tim felt the concrete rise under him. It grew, swelling higher and higher. He was going up. He shut his eyes, holding on tight. Higher and higher he went, carried up by the ballooning concrete. Around him beams and timbers cracked. Plaster poured down. He could hear glass breaking. And a long way off, the licking crackles of fire.

"Tim," Mary's voice came faintly.

"Yes."

"We're not going to -- to make it."

"I don't know."

"We're not. I can tell."

"Maybe not." He grunted in pain as a board struck his back, settling over him. Boards and plaster, covering him, burying him. He could smell the sour smell, the night air and ash. It drifted and rolled into the cellar, through the broken window.

"Daddy," Judy's voice came faintly.

"What?"

"Aren't we going back?"

He opened his mouth to answer. A shattering roar cut his words off. He jerked, tossed by the blast. Everything was moving around him. A vast wind tugged at him, a hot wind, licking at him, gnawing at him. He held on tight. The wind pulled, dragging him with it. He cried out as it seared his hands and face.

"Mary --"

Then silence. Only blackness and silence.

Cars.

Cars were stopping nearby. Then voices. And the noise of footsteps. Tim stirred, pushing the boards from him. He struggled to his feet.

"Mary." He looked around. "We're back."

The basement was in ruins. The walls were broken and sagging. Great gaping holes showed a green line of grass beyond. A concrete walk. The small rose garden. The white stucco house next door.

Lines of telephone poles. Roofs. Houses. The city. As it had always been. Every morning.

"We're back!" Wild joy leaped through him. *Back*. Safe. It was over. Tim pushed quickly through the debris of his ruined house. "Mary, are you all right?"

"Here." Mary sat up, plaster dust raining from her. She was white all over, her hair, her skin, her clothing. Her face was cut and scratched. Her dress was torn. "Are we really back?"

"Mr McLean! You all right?"

A blue-clad policeman leaped down into the cellar. Behind him two white-clad figures jumped. A group of neighbors collected outside, peering anxiously to see.

"I'm okay," Tim said. He helped Judy and Virginia up. "I think we're all okay."

"What happened?" The policeman pushed boards aside, coming over. "A bomb? Some kind of a bomb?"

"The house is a shambles," one of the white-clad interns said. "You sure nobody's hurt?"

"We were down here. In the basement."

"You all right, Tim?" Mrs Hendricks called, stepping down gingerly into the cellar.

"What happened?" Frank Foley shouted. He leaped down with a crash. "God, Tim! What the hell were you doing?"

The two white-clad interns poked suspiciously around the ruins. "You're lucky, mister. Damn lucky. There's nothing left upstairs."

Foley came over beside Tim. "Damn it man! I *told* you to have that hot water heater looked at!"

"What?" Tim muttered.

"The hot water heater! I told you there was something wrong with the cut-off. It must've kept heating up, not turned off. . ." Foley winked nervously. "But I won't say anything, Tim. The insurance. You can count on me."

Tim opened his mouth. But the words didn't come. What could he say? -- No, it wasn't a defective hot water heater that I forgot to have repaired. No, it wasn't a faulty connection in the stove. It wasn't any of those things. It wasn't a leaky gas line, it wasn't a plugged furnace, it wasn't a pressure cooker we forgot to turn off.

It's war. Total war. And not just war for me. For my family. For my house.

It's for your house, too. Your house and my house and all the houses. Here and in the next block, in the next town, the next state and country and continent. The whole world, like this. Shambles and ruins. Fog and dank weeds growing in the rusting slag. War for all of us. For everybody crowding down into the basement, white-faced, frightened, somehow sensing something terrible.

And when it really came, when the five years were up, there'd be no escape. No going back, tipping back into the past, away from it. When it came for them all, it would have them for eternity; there would be no one climbing back out, as he had.

Mary was watching him. The policeman, the neighbors, the white-clad interns -- all of them were watching him. Waiting for him to explain. To tell them what it was.

"Was it the hot water heater?" Mrs Hendricks asked timidly. "That was it, wasn't it, Tim? Things like that do happen. You can't be sure. . ."

"Maybe it was home brew," a neighbor suggested, in a feeble attempt at humor. "Was that it?"

He couldn't tell them. They wouldn't understand, because they didn't want to understand. They didn't want to know. They needed reassurance. He could see it in their eyes. Pitiful, pathetic fear. They sensed something terrible -- and they were afraid. They were searching his face, seeking his help. Words of comfort. Words to banish their fear.

"Yeah," Tim said heavily. "It was the hot water heater."

"I thought so!" Foley breathed. A sigh of relief swept through them all. Murmurs, shaky laughs. Nods, grins.

"I should have got it fixed," Tim went on. "I should have had it looked at a long time ago. Before it got in such bad shape." Tim looked around at the circle of anxious people, hanging on his words. "I should have had it looked at. Before it was too late."

www.ingramcontent.com/pod-product-compliance
Lightning Source LLC
Chambersburg PA
CBHW070808120626
46557CB00002B/763